Appointment to View
By Ryta CYN Lyndley

A CIP catalogue record for this title is available from the British Library.

Published in 2014 by Prudent Publishing Raunds UK.

ISBN 978-0-9926548-2-5

Printed & Bound in Great Britain by
Latimer Trend & Company Ltd
Estover Road, Plymouth PL6 7PY

Cover design by www.creativebeast.co.uk

Images supplied by Shutterstock

Contents

With love light and laughter

from Peta x

4

Chapter 1
A New Life Begins

Ryta's exciting life continued. No sooner had she returned from Tenerife with Robert, than she was off to Devon with Jack. Life certainly wasn't dull! She didn't realise there was another player to be added to the team! Although it was pleasant to have a fling, she didn't view either of the two relationships as long term.

She still continued to go to ceroc dancing, as it was fun and invigorating. Partners were changed every few minutes, so there was no chance of getting stuck with someone incompatible. Women as well as men were encouraged to ask each other to dance; a refusal wasn't allowed! The idea was to get everybody up off their chairs, on the floor dancing and enjoying themselves.

One evening, Ryta approached three men sitting together.

'Would one of you like to dance with me?' she enquired with a smile.

The men sat transfixed.

'Don't all rush at once!' she said encouragingly.

One of the men took her up on her offer. Little did she know this was to be the beginning of a new romance.

After the dance, Tom began his patter.

'Been dancing long?' he asked.

'What do you do for a living?' she countered.

'I'm a commercial paint sprayer,' he replied.

It also transpired that he read The Sun newspaper. Well, she was only looking for a dance partner, not a soul mate!

The evening drew to a close.

'Would you like to go for a drink? Can I have your phone number?' he asked.

'I haven't a pen,' she answered, glancing back over her shoulder, as she was talking to some friends.

Undeterred, Tom found a pen and gave Ryta his details on a scrap of paper.

Telling her friend Maureen the next day how exhilarating the dancing had been, she then asked Ryta if she would take her sister Jill, a widow, to a singles club on Saturday night.

'Oh no!' Ryta wailed. 'Not a grab-a-granny club! I never go to those events.'

'But, Ryta, you have a car, Jill hasn't, and she has lost two husbands to cancer.'

With this sobering thought, she agreed.

The evening was approaching. Ryta, despite seeing this as a good deed, thought perhaps she should have some fun and enjoyment too.

When Tom had given her the scrap of paper, little did she know she was going to ring this paint sprayer that read The Sun. We all make judgmental decisions about people and places, and she was no exception; so the deed was done, and a message left on his answer phone.

'Jill and I are going to Wood Green Animal Sanctuary to a disco. If you are up for a boogie, see you there at 8 o'clock. Don't bother to return the call. If you're there, you are, if you're not, you're not.'

Jill and Ryta arrived at the venue. There were only a few cars parked outside. They paid, entered and approached the bar. A lone female was enjoying a drink.

'Are you on your own?' Ryta asked.

'Yes,' she replied.

'You're brave, coming on your own,' Jill said.

'Well, the choice is stay at home or go out, so I came out.'

'Would you like to sit with us?' Ryta asked.

She agreed. They sat at a table near the dance floor and started to chat.

Jill glanced towards the door.

'Goodness, look at the queue. I'd better get another round of drinks in.'

She returned to the bar.

Ryta, watching Jill leave, noticed a man sitting on his own

at the table behind the two women.

'Excuse me, are you on your own?' she enquired.

'Yes,' he replied.

'Would you like to join us?' she asked.

He smiled and sat down with them.

Ryta began making introductions when a voice behind her said, 'Hello, Ryta.'

She turned, and to her surprise there stood Tom and Jake from ceroc dance class.

'Hello, you two,' she answered. 'Would you like to sit with us, or are you on the pull?'

Amid laughter and more introductions, they joined the party.

Jill returned with the drinks.

'I can't believe it!' she exclaimed. 'I've only been to buy a round of drinks and now there are three men at the table.'

'Well, I always was a fast worker,' Ryta replied with a twinkle in her eye.

The evening was a great success for everyone. Ryta danced every record with Tom or Jake to the lively music; she hoped the more she practised, the more proficient a dancer she would become.

Tom and Ryta did, however, make time to chat, starting to get to know each other. She began to realise he was a kind, caring, thoughtful individual.

Tom and Jake suggested that Ryta and Jill should visit Tom's house to play cards one evening, so a date was arranged.

When Ryta and Jill arrived at Tom's house, they were both amazed to find such a clean, tidy home for a single man. They all enjoyed their time together so another date was set for the four to go out for a meal.

After a couple of dates Ryta decided it was time to seduce Tom. She was going to Kingsthorpe for the day and asked him if Raunds was nearby, should she call in for a cup of tea. He welcomed the idea and invited her to a Sunday roast dinner.

'Can you cook?' she asked incredulously.

'I cook a roast every Sunday,' he replied with a grin.

'Well, this is a bit of a shock, a kind, thoughtful man with a clean, tidy house, who can cook; what a find!'

She arrived late, knocking on the door a little apprehensively.

As it opened she said, 'Sorry I'm late. Have you eaten the dinner or burnt it?'

'No,' he answered. 'I just turned it down.'

They stood in the kitchen, the aroma of roast dinner getting the juices going in their mouths.

'Would you like a glass of wine?' Tom asked.

Ryta smiled and said, 'Yes, please!'

They both stood contentedly sipping, when Ryta suddenly remarked, 'What's this then, feed them then fuck them?'

Tom laughed and took her hand.

'Let's forget about the dinner,' he said.

'No!' she replied. 'I want my roast pork first!'

So the scene was set.

Ryta and Tom gradually spent more time together until every weekend was enjoyed at his home. She found him very easy to live with and vice versa, and this continued for a year.

Meanwhile, Ryta's inner voice kept telling her to get on with the book.

After discussing this strange request with Tom, as she had no desire to be a writer, he suggested that she move in with him to get on with it. There wouldn't be any interruptions, as no one would know that she was living there. The phone wouldn't ring or the door be knocked upon.

'If you don't like living with me, when you have written the book you can move out again.'

In the first week she knew she had made the right decision. She knuckled down, and said, 'Okay, God, what do you want me to write about?'

Thirty thousand words and three months later, the book was complete.

It was published by her manager, Matylda, and a thousand copies printed for the first print.

In the first year, after a radio interview and a couple of mentions in local newspapers, a total of five hundred copies had been sold.

The life-changing experience was about to begin with her divorce from Mick, her now ex-husband, and a name change to Ryta C Y N Lyndley.

Chapter 2
Home from Home

A few years passed, and eventually Tom and Ryta decided to buy a house together. An estate agent was consulted, aptly named 'Appointment to View', who they met with some trepidation.

His laptop showed three different types of property: a small country cottage, a new four-bedroom detached house and a dilapidated Victorian semi with three floors. Ryta enthusiastically saw the potential in the Victorian semi for a bed and breakfast business, or, as she explained to Tom, studio apartments.

Tom felt apprehensive regarding the starting-up of a new business. At the age of 63 he had been looking forward to a more relaxed lifestyle.

They went to view all three houses, but were in for a shock when they saw the Victorian semi-detached, as there were three sitting tenants.

Ryta was not to be put off, though, her positive, bubbly personality overriding any doubts Tom might have or the problems he could foresee in the future.

'Let's go for it.'

Ryta was on a wave of optimism, imagining mentally mothering the guests (whether they wanted to be or not), who would be a substitute for the family she never had.

Tom finally gave in, seeing this prospective episode in his life as a new, fun experience rather than a penance. Little did he know that he would soon be living in a drama of his own making!

When the decision had been made to buy, Ryta and Tom popped round to the house repeatedly, discussing different ideas and formulating a plan of action, to start on day one. They decided that the seven rooms would be fully equipped with en suite shower and loo in readiness to become fully contained studio flats.

The three sitting tenants were all male, of different ages. Colonel Henshaw was the eldest; a retired soldier, his main hobby was organic gardening, and he made use of the back garden as his green allotment. He was the stereotypical army officer, with his Brylcreamed hair, well-pressed clothes and shiny shoes.

Jolly Roger was in his fifties, tall, dark and handsome, and very much a ladies' man. Twice divorced, he was once a millionaire but had lost all the money in bad business deals. However, he still embraced the high life, keeping his horse in a livery yard and running with the local hunt.

Handy Andy was the third man on the middle floor. He was a fairly quiet, thoughtful, kind individual who worked as a van driver, but with unusual hobbies, including plane and train spotting. He looked a little scruffy, with sticky-up hair before it became fashionable, and holes in his jumpers. But on Sundays, a different Andy appeared in smart grey flannels, shirt, tie and navy blazer, who joined his dad playing bowls.

All three men had had to share the combined bathroom and loo, so they were looking forward to the new individual facilities, including a Baby Belling cooker and hot plate in each room.

The mortgage had to be paid, so the well thought-out plan went into action. Bob the builder arrived to start the conversions, finding Ryta anxious to fill the rooms.

Local post offices and corner shops were, she hoped, a good bet to put up postcards advertising the rooms for rent. She did the rounds eagerly, and in no time at all the phone rang with the first enquiry.

'Hello, can I help you?' was always her initial response.

'I'm enquiring about the room. Could you please give me some more details? My name is Maddy and I'm a yoga teacher.'

Maddy was a vegan, interested in Buddhism and wrote saucy novels to supplement her income. Ryta was an animal

lover, vegetarian and interested in holistic therapies and remedies, so they immediately met on common ground. Once the
details were sorted out, Maddy said she would put a letter of
acceptance in the post and view the room when it was completed.

Ryta felt relief and excitement sweep through her all at
once. She then left to place a card in another shop that Maddy
had mentioned.

Tom was in charge, so answered the door following a timid
knock. There on the doorstep stood a stunning young lady,
with pre-Raphaelite auburn hair cascading to her shoulders,
huge eyes with inch-long lashes and a perfect cupid-bow
mouth. Wow! he thought.

'I've called about the room,' she whispered softly.

Tom quickly invited her in and showed her the downstairs
rooms, which had been earmarked for the two ladies. Terms
discussed and agreed, she was just leaving when Ryta appeared.

'What have you taken that strumpet on for? She's single,
she'll be trouble,' hissed Ryta.

'Angelina seemed very pleasant and polite,' Tom said.

'Well, it's done now; at least the mortgage is covered.'

Chapter 3
The Adventure Had Started

After the builders had finished their alterations, a new, spacious driveway was decided upon to keep the guests' cars off the road. The moulded style was chosen, but after completion the manhole cover needed to be redone. A young man arrived, and upon lifting the cover he found the sewage was backing up. Not a pretty sight!

'Have you any draining rods, love?' he asked.

'No, but I could go and buy some,' she replied.

'Here you are, you can borrow mine,' he said, feeling generous after devouring his coffee and Ryta's homemade flapjacks.

He started to rod, but nothing was moving.

'Let's have a look along the run,' he said, picking up his crowbar and moving towards a neighbour's house.

They went along two houses, peering into their drains, and found the source of the blockage. Ryta knocked on the second door, but there was no response.

'Well,' he said as he lay down his crowbar, 'we'll go back to the rodding.'

He left to finish his work, so she continued to rod.

She decided to wear a boiler suit for this mucky job and was pleased she did when she was splattered with effluence each time the rod slipped. The rod suddenly shot forward as a gush of goo moved into the next drain.

'It's moving!' she cried excitedly and prodded once more. 'Eureka!'

It was lunchtime.

'Would you like to come in for some soup and a hot roll?' she asked invitingly.

'No thanks, I'll have it in the van,' he decided.

When the drains were flowing again and Ryta was wiping and packing up the rods, he asked where his crowbar was.

Ryta knew it had been left outside, next door but one. She knocked on their door.

'Could we have the crowbar left outside your house please?' she enquired.

'Oh! I thought it was my dad's,' the lady replied.

Good try, thought Ryta.

'What were you looking down my drain for?' she asked defensively as she returned the crowbar to Ryta.

'My drain was backing up to your house, but it's clear now so we don't have to call out Dynorod.'

Meanwhile, inside the house, Angelina had moved in next door to Maddy.

Angelina had previously been living with her wealthy jeweller boyfriend in a luxurious flat, but had become fed up with his infidelities. He always tried to placate her with another diamond. The final straw was when he wanted her to join his latest floozy in a threesome romp. Enough was enough!

Ryta sat at the kitchen table, the warmth of the sun on her arm as it shone through the window, listening to the sound of the Colonel's metal fork against stones as he turned the earth over, eagerly forking for his new potatoes. At last peace and quiet; now she would be able to write the book she felt she had inside her, just waiting to burst out.

This tranquil daydreaming was replaced by the ringing of the doorbell. Ryta looked at the clock: 10.30 a.m. It must be the postman, she thought idly as she went to answer the door.

'Good morning!' she said to the postman. 'Is it warm enough for you today?'

He was dressed in his post office shorts and shirt, and his face was wearing a big smile.

'Yes, m'am,' he said. 'Would you please sign here?' He offered her his pen.

'Thank you!' Ryta said. 'Nice legs, shame about the face! Te he!'

They always had a bit of banter whenever he knocked at the door.

'What's this poster about in your window?' he said.

'Oh, that's Angelina, she's into animal rights; only free range eggs, not captive battery hens for her.'

'Pretty girl,' he said admiringly.

'Yes, stunning,' Ryta agreed, wondering if this young Jamaican postman had a soft spot for the lovely Angelina.

She signed for Jolly Roger, one of the guests, placing the letter in her pocket to give to him when he returned from work. Roger did something in the city; he never went into detail, and only spoke about his weekend life of riding with the hunt, wearing his pink jacket, and his horse Holly. Hunter Holly was kept in a livery yard nearby.

Ryta went back to her reverie in the sun. Six months ago she would never have imagined she and Tom would be looking after and running a home with lodgers, or guests' as she liked to think of them.

How life can change almost overnight, with events jumping up and hitting you over the head. Sometimes nice, sometimes nasty, but for Tom and Ryta this was becoming an extraordinary experience. Involved in five strangers' lives that were rapidly becoming like family, drawn together by circumstances, becoming closer, sometimes more so, than blood relations.

The Colonel entered the kitchen, proudly showing his freshly dug potatoes to Ryta.

'What could be better than these?' he said, perspiration running down his face.

'Hope you aren't overdoing it, Colonel,' Ryta remarked. 'Do you think you may need a little help?'

'Well, John will be joining me soon, so I'll be able to take it easy then.'

John Plonk was Irish and formally the Colonel's batman. Both retired from the army, they had lost contact but had recently bumped into each other again.

'It was good luck that Tom and John met each other in the

Tuesday pool team, wasn't it, Colonel?' Ryta said, as she looked at the vegetables. 'With all these organic vegetables we should have a social Saturday or Sunday to get to know the guests and introduce them to each other.'

A Sunday evening seemed to be a good time for them all, so Ryta decided to cook a warming vegetarian casserole, with Colonel Henshaw providing most of the vegetables from the back garden. The meal was set for 6 p.m.

The aroma of cooking filled the kitchen as one by one the guests appeared, the three men glad they were being looked after. Angelina and Maddy appeared together and were introduced to the three men, who already knew each other. They all tucked into the food, relaxed and started to chat.

'Delicious vegetables, Colonel,' Maddy said.

'Didn't realise all this food could be so tasty without meat,' commented Roger. 'I suppose I could get used to it.'

'Well, for every pound of meat you get from an animal you have to feed it 10lbs of grain, which with world grain and water shortages just isn't economic in today's world,' explained Maddy.

'People won't give up their steaks for veggie burgers,' Roger replied sardonically.

'They may have to as America puts more and more land over to biofuels to make up for the lack of oil.' She paused. 'The price of food will go up due to scarcity like is happening here, with the rise in fuel prices.'

'The nation will be thinner and healthier just like in the war, Roger. You remember that, don't you?'

'I do!' interrupted the Colonel. 'There was community spirit then. Folk all worked together, the army sorted out the scroungers and layabouts, bit of discipline needed, in fact a lot of discipline needed for some.' His gaze turned towards Andy.

Andy was oblivious, debating whether he should request another helping to keep him going for the next two days.

'Can anyone manage some more?' Ryta asked.

'Thought you'd never ask,' Andy replied with a smile, loading his plate.

These weekly dinners continued as the guests got to know each other. Sometimes a guest missed a week or misheard what was on the menu, which on one occasion was rather a surprise to the others.

Angelina, passing Andy on the stairs one day, asked, 'Have you any idea what's on the menu this Sunday, Andy?'

'Thai,' he replied as he ran out of the front door to work.

Black tie, she thought as she lay soaking in the bath, visualising herself in a long dress, with the men in their dinner jackets. It would be a nice change, to make an event of it.

The following Sunday Angelina spent time on her make-up and painting her fingernails, ensuring she was dressed to kill! After dressing in a long scarlet dress, elbow-length black gloves and a sparkly tiara in her hair, she decided to arrive late and make an entrance. And she certainly did, being the only one dressed to the nines. She looked amazing!

The men's eyes lit up.

'Where are you taking us, Angelina?'

She was astonished to find they were still in their jeans.

'Andy said it was black tie,' she said.

'No! Thai as in Thai food; very tasty but you look pretty tasty to us,' Andy replied.'

She joined in their laughter.

'Oh dear, it was a play on words. I'll go and change into my jeans.'

'No, you look lovely,' said Ryta. 'Stay as you are; we can all admire you while we eat our dinner.'

'You do look good enough to eat!' Roger remarked, leering across the table. 'Will you be my pudding?'

Laughter filled the kitchen. They all enjoyed their time on a Sunday; it was becoming like a weekly party.

'Yes, my dear, you look very fetching!' the Colonel remarked.

He then turned to Maddy to enquire how her yoga classes were progressing. She told him they were going very well, but she was about to start as a pupil in a new pole dancing class. The men all spoke in unison, their minds picturing images of scantily dressed girls gyrating around a pole to music.

'Will you be the oldest pole dancer in town?' Roger drawled.

'It's not seedy,' she said defensively. 'It's very tasteful and good fun, so I'm told.'

'You are only as young as the woman you feel,' was Roger's final remark.

'Now, now, I'm sure it will be fun for all,' Ryta interjected, and then changed the topic of conversation back to the delicious Thai food they were all enjoying.

'You're quiet tonight, Tom,' Maddy said.

'Yes, that ex-wife of mine has been on the phone again.'

'What does she want now?' Maddy enquired. 'More of your worldly goods?'

'Not many of those left. This time half an insurance policy.'

'Tell her where to go, Tom. Be strong.'

'I'm trying to be,' he said, with a resigned look on his face.

The meal finished with, there was more jesting.

'It's a pleasure to live with such a jolly crowd,' Ryta told Tom later.

He was quiet, pondering the problem of Cowell.

'I don't want to give her any money,' he told Ryta. 'She gave her word that she wouldn't claim half of the policy.'

'She always had a problem with telling the truth,' Ryta replied.

Chapter 4
Tom's Story

Tom and his brother Dave lived with their parents, Win and Charles, in a London terraced house. The building was damp and cold, as there was no central heating in those days. When it was icy, there was frost on the inside of the windows, and sometimes Tom would curl up in a ball with his hands between his knees trying to keep warm, before finally dropping off to sleep in the cosy flannelette sheets.

His mum was widowed before marrying Charles. She was vivacious and fun loving, playing the piano and singing in pubs, always laughing heartily – the life and soul of the party. He was quieter, an anchor to her uplifting presence, trying to keep her feet on the ground, with little success.

They were both very happy, and their two sons cemented their union. Children sometimes drive their parents mad, and these two were no exception. Every Sunday afternoon the parents went upstairs for a lie down, leaving the boys to their own devices. One day they came downstairs to find that every clock and watch in the house had been taken apart and the insides displayed proudly on the kitchen table.

They were lively, happy, healthy boys until one day Tom found he had an abscess in his ear. Eventually, it cleared up, but unfortunately it left him with a hearing defect. This wasn't picked up at school, and the teachers just thought he was a bit slow compared to his brother Dave. Nevertheless, when he left school he started his first job as a paint sprayer, which he continued for the next forty-five years.

Tom and Dave, like any other young men, did the rounds of the pubs and dance halls at that time. Tottenham Royal, The Athenaeum at Muswell Hill and The Cambridge on the North Circular Road, Edmonton were a few of their favourite haunts to pull the birds. They soon succeeded, and both found themselves a bride.

Tom married Yvonne at the age of twenty-two, a pretty, sensitive girl, fair skinned with auburn hair. She was well spoken and had been brought up with good manners, and Tom was her little bit of rough! He fathered three daughters, which he felt was the best thing that had ever happened in his life, but sadly it was to end.

Yvonne was a stay-at-home wife, her job being to care, cook and look after the whole family. Tom's role was the breadwinner, working all hours to feed the family. One day Yvonne mentioned that as this was the 1980s, perhaps the deeds of their home should be put in both their names. Tom readily agreed to this request, seeing no reason to deny his wife, as she was a good woman who had worked hard to ensure the girls grew up to be well mannered, happy individuals.

One day, out of the blue and much to Tom's astonishment, Yvonne told him she wanted a divorce. After twenty years of knowing, loving and feeling close to this person, he couldn't believe she had dropped this bombshell; it couldn't be happening to him. He had envisaged they would spend the rest of their lives together.

Yvonne departed with her new beau, leaving Tom with two of the three daughters. He was finding it very difficult to cope with a job, the shopping, running a home and being responsible for the two girls. His eldest daughter Sally even taught him to iron; he discovered it was, according to her, 'a new man' skill.

Yvonne remarried, taking the youngest of the three daughters with her. It was then that Tom finally realised his marriage was over. Rather than giving in to despair, he decided to take control of his life and return to the social scene.

He was quickly snapped up by Cowell, a tarty divorcee, who, although married to husband number four, wasn't averse to a bit on the side! Sometimes men don't always think with their brains, and in time Tom became husband number five.

He went like a lamb to the slaughter, taking on her three noisy sons. What a contrast to the well-behaved, considerate daughters he'd left behind.

He managed to stay the course for thirteen years, dealing en route with a drug addict son, who punched holes in doors and stole cash and credit cards to fund his habit. Life was never meant to be easy in this household. An older son habitually jumped out of the bedroom window, landing on the garage roof, and shinned down the drainpipe, escaping to freedom. Tom's cars were not his own, often returning in a worse condition than they went out in!

When Cowell and Tom went on holiday to Antigua, this was to be their swansong. On their return, she moved out. Tom had to put his hand in his pocket and shell out for another half a house. Once, but not twice; this was becoming a habit!

Tom was rattling around in his three-bedroom home when Jake arrived. Jake was also suffering from matrimonial problems and had decided to seek a refuge; Tom had the accommodation, and a friendship was formed. Jake's hobby was ceroc dancing, so Tom joined him. He found it fun, so they began going out dancing together on a regular basis.

Five years passed, with various ladies appearing and disappearing until one evening, Tom met Ryta.

Tom used to be a paint sprayer until he was unlawfully sacked from his job at the age of sixty-three. He hadn't been happy in his employment as a result of being bullied, together with an African man named John. Tom and John were repeatedly told they were old, slow and stupid; as Tom had been employed there for ten years, this was clearly untrue.

Things came to a head one day when one of the younger members, Lionel, challenged Tom in their lunch break to an arm wrestle. Tom had very strong muscles and won the contest. The younger man angrily swung him round, and a nasty cracking sound came from Tom's knee. He didn't collapse, but it was enough to stop the onslaught from a man at 6'4' to Tom's 5'6'.

Ryta arrived at Tom's home later that evening to find him dragging one leg.

'What's happened? Have you had an accident? We're supposed to be going to Devon tomorrow.'

'I'll be able to drive,' Tom replied.

'Not with a leg like that,' she answered.

Tom told her the tale, and then, with six magnets fastened around his ballooning knee, they went to bed.

'Did you fill in an accident report?' Ryta asked the next day as they travelled to Devon; the swelling had gone down overnight and his leg was much improved.

He admitted that it hadn't been mentioned.

They had an enjoyable weekend, with Tom returning to work on the Monday.

When he came in for his dinner that evening, Ryta asked, 'Was your accident entered in the accident book?'

'No, the boss wasn't there. The foreman said it was only horseplay. I don't think they want to be bothered with it.'

'Well, ask again tomorrow; sometimes there are long-term repercussions, so it's better to get it down in writing.'

Tuesday was a rerun of Monday. No one was interested in someone considered old, slow and stupid. The harassment continued, with Lionel chipping away at Tom's confidence, saying he'd be out of a job next week.

ACAS was called for some advice on victimisation, and it was suggested that Tom should join a union, which he did. ACAS also recommended instigating the grievance procedure. A letter was typed in readiness to be given to Douglas, the boss.

The next day whenTom arrived for work Lionel cornered him.

'We may not sort this out on the premises, but I'm going to sort it out between you and me.'

Feeling threatened, Tom decided not to give the letter to Douglas.

The next day, the threats continued.

'If you were not such an old man, I'd put one on you,' Lionel said when there was no one around to overhear him. 'You'll be out next week.'

Tom had his mortgage to pay, so these comments were niggling away at him, disturbing his sleep.

A further grievance procedure was typed and both letters were popped through the letterbox where Douglas lived, for him to find when he returned from his weekend away.

Monday dawned, and Tom and Lionel were called together. Lionel said it had all been a joke and Douglas insisted they both shake hands and forget the whole thing.

On Tuesday, Ryta was at home when the phone rang.

'Would you come and be a witness, as Douglas wants to discuss the letters?'

'I'll be there in twenty minutes,' she replied.

She dressed carefully in a smart business suit, as she wanted to look professional. She wasn't going to be treated as though she was old, slow and stupid!

Present at the meeting were Douglas, Dwayne the foreman, Tom and Ryta. Ryta sat composed, with a notepad and pen ready. Douglas started.

'We've discussed the letters. Are you happy with that?'

'No, Lionel has been bullying me,' Tom answered.

Douglas said, 'You've shaken hands and moved swiftly on.'

Dwayne said, 'You do not do the job right.'

Douglas continued, 'I've told you to wear glasses, but I'm not going to give you a warning. Why didn't you come to me about the bullying? I've had to put in another £20,000 from my pension fund to keep the business going.'

Tom said, 'I came to see you and you told me to go away.'

Ryta interrupted at that point.

'Another incident was that Dwayne said to Tom, "I don't care if it costs Douglas £5,000, you have got to go!"'

Ryta pointed her finger at Dwayne and asked if he denied saying that.

His eyes narrowed angrily and he hissed through his teeth, 'No! I don't deny saying it, I want him gone!'

'There you are,' Ryta said to Douglas.

He did not reply.

The business then began to suffer due to a decline in work to be done, so Lionel left the company. Tom and Ryta went on holiday in the November, and on Tom's return to work on the Monday he was promptly sacked. No warning, he was just told he wasn't wanted any more.

He arrived home an hour later, shocked.

'I've been sacked.'

'What good news,' Ryta said calmly. 'You are in a union.'

'But I'm sixty-three,' he replied.

He called the union office, explanations were given and a meeting was arranged with their representative.

It was all dealt with calmly. The next step was to take the company to a tribunal. The date was arranged. Then a letter addressed to Tom (as a former employee) was received from the Liquidation Department requesting numerous details.

Deciding to enlighten this government body with a few points that may have slipped the mind of Tom's old boss, Ryta phoned to ask if they were aware that this was the second occasion Douglas had gone bankrupt.

The first time she explained he had also sacked an employee, with no warning, notice or redundancy payments. This employee consulted a no win, no fee solicitor and reputedly received £20,000 for his trouble.

There was also the fact that the premises had been sold to the large business next door, so she was able to give them all the details of the purchaser. This information was of great interest, as they were unaware that Douglas was being economical with the truth.

The day of the tribunal approached. Two days before it was due to commence it was cancelled, so it was over in a flash; the truth prevailed.

Tom duly received his redundancy payment, including an

additional payment for not being given any notice. If you have worked for ten years you are entitled to ten weeks' notice.

In November 2006 Tom received a surprise phone call from Cowell.

'Hello, how are you?'

The usual pleasantries were made while Ryta anticipated a request.

'Tom, that endowment you have coming out soon; I need my half, as I'm a bit short of cash.'

'But you gave your word that you wouldn't claim on that ten years ago when we were divorced. I need it to pay my mortgage off … I was made redundant,' he replied.

'The policy is in joint names, so legally I am entitled to half of the £7,000,' she said smoothly.

'Cowell, you know I paid all the premiums from my account,' he stuttered.

'Yes, I know, but I am entitled to half.'

'You're not getting it. Goodbye,' Tom said, and put the phone down.

During 2007 Tom repeatedly tried to resolve the problem, but the insurance company would not budge. They said it is irrelevant who pays the premiums; it is the names that are on the policy that matter.

At this time Tom was a fit and healthy old age pensioner, often walking or cycling five miles a day. One sunny evening he went out on his bike, and after half an hour he had still not returned. Ryta began to wonder where he was when a motorbike pulled up and a young man approached the front door.

'Hello! Is this 41?' he asked.

'Yes,' she replied.

'Your husband has had a stroke on the mere,' he said.

'Thank you for telling me,' she said as she grabbed the car keys from the lock in the front door and left the house.

Quickly following the motorbike along a single-track road, she soon arrived at Tom's side.

'Smile, put your tongue out and lift each arm,' she ordered, remembering what she had read about strokes.

He completed these actions, and then the man on the motorbike started to help him towards the car.

Another car had stopped behind Ryta.

'Sorry to keep you waiting my husband has had a stroke,' she said to the driver.

'Can I help? I'm a nurse,' was the reply.

'Do you want to look at him or shall I take him straight to Kettering General?'

'Straight to hospital,' the nurse answered.

When they arrived, she ran into Accident and Emergency to ask for assistance. A wheelchair and helper materialised and Tom was taken into a separate room, where he was immediately hooked up to several monitors. Ryta told the various doctors and nurses that he had had a stroke, but this information was ignored. Staff came and went until 11 p.m., when a doctor said that he would need to be kept under observation overnight on an assessment ward, and asked if she could come back tomorrow.

Arriving home, she rang two friends, a hypnotherapist and a kinesiologist, to ask their advice.

The next day the diagnosis of a stroke was confirmed, with complete loss of mobility in his left arm and leg. What a shock for Tom, who was used to being so active.

Ryta started giving Tom Reiki healing twice a day and Bach flower remedies to counteract the trauma, as his body had gone into shock.

His daughter Sally arrived, so Ryta took a break and went for a coffee. When she returned half an hour later, there was an elderly grey-haired man in the bed. Goodness, these strokes age folk fast, she thought, and then noticed the man in the next bed had also disappeared.

She approached the nurses' station.

'I've only been for a coffee and Mr Homming has disappeared from his bed.'

'Yes, he has been transferred to Naseby Ward.'

She went to find him. This was a secure ward, and special buttons had to be pushed to get in and out.

'Do people escape from here?' she asked a nurse.

'They try to.'

'I'm not surprised,' she said, viewing the rows and rows of stroke victims hooked up to intravenous feeding and saline drips, lying like corpses in their beds.

Tom was sitting up awkwardly, hanging on to the bed guard. But he was smiling, which was an encouraging sign.

The next day he was visited by two physiotherapists, so his rehabilitation began.

He overheard one nurse say to another, 'He'll never be the same again.'

He told Ryta and said, 'Yes, I will! I am determined to walk and dance again.'

In three weeks and three days he walked the length of the bed, encouraged by the physiotherapist, while Ryta watched emotionally, tears running down her face.

Such progress seemed to be very rare, so the doctors and other medical personnel came to take a look at this unusual patient.

Kettering General was Tom's home for three weeks, as there were no beds available at Wellingborough Isebrook Hospital for his rehabilitation. When he was eventually transferred, he explained to the physiotherapist that he would walk out of there, as leaving in a wheelchair was not an option!

Stroke patients sometimes seem to give up and feel they don't have anything to offer in life. Two men, both younger than Tom, gave up and died. One young man was married to a pretty, caring young wife and had a daughter. Although he was fortunate to have family support with a super electronic wheelchair with a keypad in the arm of the chair, this didn't stop him from slipping into severe depression and giving up on life.

Now Tom was a resident in Wellingborough, he had his own private room rather than being on a public ward. Ryta was pleased that he was so positive, walking and feeling very much like his old self. They missed their cuddles, and decided to check if everything was still in working order. Tom assured Ryta it was, but not wanting to miss an opportunity, they decided to shut the door. There were no locks, but six weeks is a long time without a cuddle. Ryta quickly whisked off her trousers and leapt onto the bed. While they were happily checking their working parts, the door began to open. There was a mirror on the wall opposite the door, so the nurse had a surprising view.

'Just give us five minutes,' Tom called out.

The nurse obligingly closed the door.

A little bit of what you fancy does you good. Ryta's healing was helping Tom with his rehabilitation, and although satisfying, it was not yet available on the National Health Service.

After starting his physiotherapy Tom had an appointment with his consultant, who chatted to him for an hour and a half. When Ryta arrived later, she was amazed that he had been allowed that long; usually you're lucky if you get five minutes.

Tom explained they had discussed the speed of his progress in four weeks, and also about the benefits of yoga, Bach flower remedies, hypnotherapy and kinesiology. The consultant asked if Ryta would consider giving Reiki healing to other stroke patients, and she agreed to give her time free of charge. Sadly, when it was put before a panel of hospital experts, her offer was declined.

Tom's speedy progress was considered a rare occurrence and some doctors and medical personnel came to visit him, monitoring his progress.

During this period of hospitalisation, friends called on Ryta or phoned to enquire about his welfare. She answered the front door to one good friend who asked how Tom was. She invited him in, and to her surprise he grabbed hold of her bottom and made his intentions quite clear. She wasn't having any of this nonsense and promptly asked him to leave. He was walking down the drive when he dropped what Ryta thought was a handkerchief. She called out his name and he stopped. She ran down the drive to pick up the hankie and found it was a French letter out of its packet.

'You dropped this,' Ryta said.

'No, it's not mine,' he replied.

'Yes it is, you've just dropped it,' she said as she handed it to him.

He took it, looking embarrassed upon realising that he had been caught out.

Three months later, Tom left Wellingborough after a home visit to ensure he was able to make a cup of tea and get in and out of the bath unaided.

The follow-up physiotherapy involved one outpatient session per week. One of his major achievements was a five-mile walk on Boxing Day; his Christmas present to himself!

Tom became interested in spirituality as opposed to religion after meeting Ryta. He had thought that being spiritual was about being in harmony with nature, including kindness to other people, animals and insects. In his opinion the mainstream religions seemed to want to browbeat folk into submission with their dogmas. Catholics had not had very good press for centuries due to not encouraging people to have a choice over birth control and the covering up of bad deeds by priests. The Anglican Church is bigoted, with no women vicars allowed, which is probably adding to their demise. Life is constantly changing, and we must change with it or be left behind.

During this period Tom was only in contact with one of his daughters, Susie, who lived in the USA.

She used to visit him, and on one occasion they both decided to see a medium for a reading. Tom was told by the medium he would be reunited with his daughter Sally, whom he had fallen out with several years before, at Christmas time, as the medium could see Christmas trees and baubles.

Two years later, the phone rang in early December, and Ryta answered to find it was Sally asking to speak to her dad. They were reunited after fifteen years of silence. He came off the phone and wept tears of joy. He had always sent cards, but never knew if they were received or binned.

On another occasion while having a reading, the medium told him he had four children in his first marriage. He disagreed, saying he had three. He was told that his wife had a miscarriage, and that it was a boy. Tom confirmed this was correct. The medium continued by saying that his son had grown up in the spirit world and had been with Tom on his path through life, but his work was now complete.

Chapter 5
Independence for Cornwall?

Ryta and Tom went on a welcome holiday to Cornwall and Devon. The management and staff were, as always, welcoming and hospitable. They lived in one of those parts of the country that didn't appear to suffer from stress. On the roads, old cars were driven without any thoughts about having the latest, newest coupé. To Cornish folk it was only about getting from A to B in a roadworthy vehicle. The registration plate was not an issue, and they were happy to be healthy and living in such a beautiful place. They considered they were fortunate to be living in one of the least populated, most stunning parts of the country, with the sea only a few miles away.

Ryta and Tom sat at Watergate Bay, eating their freshly caught fish, and with the amazing view, watching the surfers swoop in front of them, what could be better? Only the two-mile walk along the beach afterwards to walk off the extra calories, and to return for organic cake and tea!

Chapter 6
A New Arrival

They returned home refreshed, so the next day, after a social Sunday, Ryta was back to writing at the kitchen table. Then the doorbell rang.

Not the postman today! she thought. Wrong time.

Smiling, she opened the door.

A young punk-looking man stood on the doorstep, with dark, spiky hair in cerise stripes, one ear holding several earrings, 'Peace' tattooed across his right hand, and wearing a fringed leather jacket and a red and white scarf around his neck.

'Hello, can I help you?' she asked.

'Hello, I'm Tyler, I've come to stay with my brother.'

'Your brother?' Ryta asked, wondering if she had forgotten a guest's instruction.

'Yes,' he said. 'Roger … I sent him a letter.'

'Oh, my giddy aunt!' she said. 'I remember it arriving. Was it Recorded Delivery?'

He nodded.

'But I can't remember giving it to him. Do come in.'

They walked along the hall to the kitchen.

'Would you like a drink?' she asked as she reached towards the kettle. 'Tea or coffee?'

'Coffee please, white no sugar,' he said as he sat at the kitchen table.

She filled the kettle, trying to think quickly. Where had she put the letter? In a safe place but where?

The young man didn't appear to bear any resemblance to his brother Roger, who always looked like a tailor's dummy in his immaculate pinstripe suit.

'Why didn't you text him?' Ryta asked. Young people always had mobile phones stuck to their ears.

'No money to buy a card,' he groaned. 'So my friend paid

for the postage. Better really, as Roger and I fell out a long time ago.'

The sound of someone working in the garden came through the window.

'Oh, do you have a gardener?'

'No, that's the Colonel. He's retired and very interested in organic gardening.'

'I recently lived in a commune. Can I go and have a look?'

'Yes of course. Would you like to take him a mug too?'

Both mugs on the tray, he left the kitchen. Ryta heard the sound of Omo, the Colonel's dog, barking and knew Tyler must have found the Colonel. She thought about leaving the kitchen to go upstairs to check the pockets of her clothes for the letter. Where was Tyler going to sleep? She'd better make some decisions.

In the garden, Tyler said, 'Hello, Colonel, here's your tea.'

'Thank you! Who are you?'

'I'm Tyler, Roger's brother.'

'Didn't know he had a brother, but I can see a slight family resemblance. Where have you come from?'

'I've been working in a commune, but I need to get a job, as I've run out of money. I hope my brother may have some ideas or contacts.'

'People always need gardeners; have you given that any thought?'

In the kitchen, Angelina appeared and asked Ryta if she could have a word.

'Although I haven't been here long, I am very happy, but have decided to give it another go with my boyfriend, Jeff. He wants me to give him a second chance, so I will have to give you my notice.'

Well, every cloud has a silver lining, Ryta thought One out one in.

'How soon can you leave?' Ryta asked. 'Not that I'm trying to push you out.'

'Well,' she sighed, 'he said he wants me back in his arms as soon as possible.'

'What about tonight? Can he wait that long?'

With the Tyler crisis solved, Angelina declined to take any of the furniture this time, since she hoped it was for good. So Tyler had his furnished studio flat; what a stroke of luck. There was only the problem of the disagreement between Roger and Tyler to sort out. Surely it couldn't have been too serious.

With some anxious thoughts, Ryta waited for Roger to return from the city.

'Hello, Roger! Your brother Tyler arrived today.'

'What does he want?' he asked with a frown. 'Has he got a job?'

'No, he was rather hoping you could help him find a position.'

They both walked towards the kitchen.

'Sit down, Roger, and have a nice cup of tea. Tyler is in the garden with the Colonel at the moment, where he has been all afternoon giving him a hand with the heavy digging.'

'Would you two like another cup?' she called out of the window to the happy gardeners, who, despite the difference in age, seemed to be getting on very well.

This time it was Roger's turn to go outside with the tea tray.

'Hello, bruv!' said Tyler. 'Sorry you didn't get the letter.'

'What letter?'

On hearing this, Ryta rushed into the garden and said, 'I'm really sorry, Roger, I put the letter in a safe place for you, but being a dippy old age pensioner, I forgot where that was.'

'No worries,' said Roger.

With the Colonel as referee, the two brothers settled their dispute, and Tyler was told that this would be a good place to hang up his hat. Now just the problem of a paid occupation remained. Roger took Ryta to one side to confirm that he would foot the bill for Tyler's rent for one month, to ease him into his responsibilities.

'Oh, Roger, you are all heart,' Ryta said. 'You have a hard exterior, but a soft centre.'

'Well, don't you go getting the wrong impression of me. I don't want you ruining my reputation!' he retorted with a wink and a smile.

Another Sunday! Where had that week gone?

This week it was veggie pie with a puff pastry lid in veggie gravy, prepared by Maddy. Now there was a new face around the table, Tyler. Angelina's sudden departure was explained and good wishes sent her way, hoping she would find happiness. Meanwhile, Tyler had been working hard door knocking and placing cards in shop windows to advertise his hourly rates, with some success.

He had acquired three jobs by knocking on the doors of houses with overgrown gardens and was welcomed by three elderly people who were now his employers. They were delighted with his youth, enthusiasm and, hopefully, horticultural skills. Roger was impressed by his brother's initiative and had put out some feelers himself.

Tyler was appreciative and said 'I may have need of a job inside in the winter months, if the work outside comes to a halt.'

The Colonel had been on the allotment waiting list for a while and was fortunate to be given a vacant plot. John Plonk played pool every week in a team with Tom, so when they were chatting about John being in the services, they found out he used to be the Colonel's batman. John was Irish and until recently had worked on a turkey farm. He informed Tom of his responsibilities, and said that the turkeys were kept inside and not given the choice to run free. They were so overweight they couldn't mate and sadly they had to be masturbated by John and the other workers until their semen could be sucked up a straw and then injected into the female turkeys.

'Bet you're glad you're not a turkey, Tom,' he said as he saw the look of disbelief on Tom's face.

'Was this what you had to do as part of your job?' Tom asked incredulously.

'Yes,' said John. 'I must admit, I wasn't sorry when they decided to close.'

The Colonel employed John on a 'cash in hand' basis, as he would have been unable to eat if his council tax rebate and other allowances were eliminated. It suited them both, so they were both happy about the reconciliation brought about, unwittingly, by Tom.

John and the Colonel met at the allotment, where John planted everything in straight rows, with a circumference measured so that the plants were exactly the right distance apart. Whilst John toiled, the Colonel sat and watched, planning the next crop and enjoying his smoked salmon, cream cheese and chive sandwiches, while John ate his cheese and onion doorsteps in companiable silence!

The Colonel felt it was a good life, and gave others the opportunity to enjoy his organic vegetables. Now he just had to find some appreciative customers for his produce.

This was another topic for discussion over the social Sunday dinner.

The Colonel was always reading up on organic growing tips and thinking about how to reduce his expenses, and once he read that human wee could be used instead of garotta for rotting down the compost. This could be a real saving, free wee!

He decided to get himself a second-hand freezer box from a charity shop to use as his chamber pot, which he could safely carry down the stairs without spillage.

Ryta, also interested in recycling everything, even husbands, was given a second-hand computer and printer, which she received with grateful perplexity. When Tom returned from his part-time job as a car valet, she showed it to him.

'I can switch it on, but that's about all at the moment. Can't get rid of the blinking fish on the screen; still, it will be more entertaining than a goldfish bowl.'

He mentioned there were free computer classes for adults in the area, and said she should look into it.

'What a good idea,' she agreed, and resolved to phone them the next day.

She was soon attending twice a week for two hours. She found it tiring, but interesting. She was also surprised to find herself sitting next to eighty year olds, who were very au fait with this modern device and had come along to extend their knowledge to spreadsheets so they could do the accounts at their local clubs. Well, if an eighty year old could cope, then so could she.

It was difficult to practise on the computer she had at home, as different models had different options, but she wasn't about to give in. She knew she had to learn this new skill.

That night both Tom and Ryta went dancing. It was always good fun, so they decided to return to ceroc on a regular basis. Ryta was reminiscing about her first time, and she re-membered approaching the venue with trepidation, but as soon as she heard the music it was as though her soul had come home. Her spirit soared and she felt so vibrant and alive. Although she had not learnt a step, it was in that mo-ment that her heart began to sing.

Her legs were stiff and her arms worked like very old-fash-ioned train signals, in two positions, up or down. Trying to co-ordinate her arms, legs, hands and feet was like learning to drive; mirror, signal, then manoeuvre.

Her passion overcame any misgivings she had and the moves began to synchronise, her limbs and face beginning to relax and the terror retreating from her staring eyeballs. The rigid robot was replaced with a human being again, and she started to move with a vague sense of rhythm; she hoped the style would come with practice.

Partners were exchanged every few minutes so there was

no chance of spotting the inexperienced. A dazzling smile worked every time, even if his foot was pinned to the floor at that particular moment!

One of the dancing policies was never to refuse a dance, so the experts had to help the fledglings repeat the only three moves they remembered. Very tedious for those who liked to spin and twirl with what seemed a terrifying speed to the novices, who could hardly remember their left from their right.

Eventually, as with everything, practice makes perfect; arms relaxed and feet moved of their own accord. The smiles were genuine, not a caricature!

One day when Tom and Ryta were shopping in Waitrose, they were passing the TV department when on a big 40-inch screen they saw Annie Lennox singing Sweet Dreams.

Ryta wiggled her hips and said, 'Do you want to boogie, babe?'

They put their baskets down and swung into ceroc dancing, which is like ballroom jive. Three assistants working at the nearby coffee bar all rested their elbows on the counter, their chins in their hands, smiles on their faces, transfixed! They danced until the record finished and the three assistants clapped enthusiastically. Tom did a little bow and Ryta curtsied; then they picked up their baskets and continued with their shopping.

Ryta, always full of spontaneity and joy, loved to dance; she felt it was good for the soul and she danced everywhere as long as it didn't upset other people.

Chapter 7
Elsie's Tale

Ryta's mum, Elsie, now in her eighties, had begun to feel that a three-bedroom house was too much to look after. It had been fine when her and Ted had moved there twenty years ago to be near their two sons and the grandchildren. They were able to help out with babysitting when the four grandchildren were younger to give the parents a rest. Meanwhile, her daughter Ryta and her husband Mick had been busy running a pub for sixteen years, with very little spare time.

They enjoyed their grandchildren's company, but children grow up quickly, filling their lives with other interests, and they forget about their ageing grandparents, even if they aren't grumpy old men and women!

Life went on. They had their own interests, and belonged to an Old Age Pensioners Club where Ted was the treasurer. He organised holidays and trips to the coast for their friends. Eventually, Ted died at the age of eighty-two; he was better off without the pain that was caused to him by for his worn-out aorta. He would have been pleased to see the good turnout at his funeral, although he would probably have said they all came just for the free lunch!

The number of club members, most of whom were in their eighties, dwindled as they died off, and it had to be kept going by some of the younger old age pensioners; but perhaps they felt too old, too arthritic, too asthmatic to contemplate organising such a jolly club.

Lots of folk don't seem to have the motivation, though we all have a choice whether we wake up and say, 'God, another lovely day!' or, 'God, not another day!' Wake up, say thanks, I am fit, well and healthy, and you will be. Say I am in pain, old and miserable, and that's what you'll be; you can be controlled by your thoughts, positive or negative, the choice is yours.

Eventually, Ryta's mum put her house on the market and had lots of viewers. Some said nothing and just rushed into each room, had a quick look round and left. Perhaps they were prospective buy-to-rent people. Others would take their time visualising where their personal belongings would go, complimenting her on how clean and well maintained the property was. Elsie was a Leo: organised, hardworking and very tidy.

The contracts were to be exchanged with Mrs Kosovoo, a Nigerian lady who was over the moon with the property, especially as Elsie was leaving a lot of the furniture behind. Ryta started planning her mum's leaving party with the Kosovoos, introducing them to the neighbours. It was to be a lively event, and Ryta was imagining reggae music and the Kosovoos limbo dancing in the lounge, encouraging everyone else to have a go at limboing under her mum's old clothesline they'd found in the shed. Elsie wasn't sure whether her creaky neighbours with their bad backs, limpy legs and knackered knees would be able to make it through the front door, let alone shine at limbo dancing!

Ryta, not to be put off, planned the spicy curries and fresh fruit desserts; no junk food to be seen. She was looking forward to the imaginary limbo dancing to put her yoga flexibility to the test.

But it was not to be. Mrs Kosovoo was not allowed a mortgage, so it was back to the drawing board, looking for another purchaser.

Mrs Jones was looking for a clean, decorated house to let, and thought Elsie's was perfect.

Would everything go through without a hitch this time? Elsie started giving away her furniture to her appreciative neighbours.

A few weeks went by, and Mrs Jones phoned Elsie to confirm everything was under control. Elsie had heard all this before, though, so another appointment was made to view. This time it was an Asian family; the wife was pretty, very quiet and wore a colourful sari. It transpired that they had recently taken over the nearby corner shop, but felt the flat above may be a little cramped for their children, who needed a garden for them to let off steam. Elsie explained that there was already a lady in the pipeline, but she was willing to sell to whoever could raise the money first.

She asked if the shop was busy, and the husband replied, 'My wife and eldest son run the shop; I work as a prison warder.'

'Oh!' she said. 'I wondered what the initials on your jacket stood for, OHMS.'

'On Her Majesty's Service,' he replied. 'Or in prison, my fellow warders jokingly say it stands for Only Hindus, Muslims and Sikhs.'

He shook with laughter. We all like a joke, don't we?

Mrs Jones was the eventual purchaser of the property.

The house Elsie was moving into was owned by Ryta; having been purchased with her divorce settlement. When Ryta and Mick divorced, they split everything down the middle, with no recriminations and no bad feelings. At first Ryta felt she should blow the money on a Porsche, and she and Tom had visited the nearest Porsche garage in Tom's old Cavalier. This arrival did not spark any interest from the bored sales operatives, and nobody offered them any assistance. They looked at the beautiful cars, Ryta stroking the long bonnets appreciatively and wondering how she would manage to park such a lengthy beast! She liked the sound of the Porsche Club and their meetings, but as no help was forthcoming she decided to abandon the whole idea. The moral of this story is you can't judge a book by its cover.

Elsie wasn't disappointed by this tale, and said that as they weren't going to buy a posh sports car, did they think they could buy her a small bungalow near them instead.

'You said you would look after me when I got old, and I am old now,' she said.

Ryta didn't hesitate, as there was a property on their road for sale, and it was duly purchased.

Elsie had been given a new bed by one of her sons, and she had already purchased a settee and armchair for the lounge, so she was looking forward to the move. Her sons moved any remaining pieces of furniture in a van on the day. Her new life was beginning, and just down the road from Ryta and Tom.

Ryta and Tom were settled into their new life, and it was time for Ryta's mum to visit.

'How have you been, mum?'

'Fine, apart from a bit of backache but I have been to see the doctor.' She then told them the whole story from the very first phone call.

'Could I have an appointment today, please?'

'Sorry, I have no vacant appointments.'

'I have backache and I am eighty-seven years old.'

'Perhaps you could ring back at 1.30 p.m. We may have had a cancellation.'

'Okay!'

She rang back at 1.30 p.m.

'I was asked to ring back to see if there has been a cancellation?'

'No, sorry.'

'I have backache and I am eighty-seven.'

'I'll book you into the acute clinic at 3 p.m.'

'Thank you.'

3 p.m. at the clinic's reception.

'Which doctor do you have an appointment with?'

'Don't know. I have an appointment with the acoustic clinic.'

The receptionist laughed.

'I think you mean the acute clinic,' she said, and sent her along to Dr Macgaritty's room.

Elsie entered, smiled and said, 'Oh hello, it's you again!

Are you the acute clinic? I asked the lady for the acoustic clinic.'

'Were those pills I gave you so good that you are singing and dancing now?' he asked with a twinkle in his eye.

'No, my back still hurts, that's why I've come back.'

The following week she returned to the doctor again.

'What doctor are you seeing?'

'Dr Charity.'

'Do you mean Dr Macgaritty?'

'Oh yes, that's it!'

Ryta was howling with laughter. Her mum wore a hearing aid and didn't always hear everything correctly. After this latest episode Ryta suggested she wear two hearing aids to help balance her hearing.

'Oh no,' she replied, 'I don't want to hear everything in stereo. I do have a problem, though,' she said, and pulled a brown envelope from her pocket.

Chapter 8
Another Social Sunday at Home

Jolly Roger had an amazing chemistry with Maddy, but she was vegan and Roger went fox hunting.

'What are you cooking for us this Sunday, Roger, as the three of us are going to be out all day on an animal rights protest? It will be handy for us to have a meal ready for when we get back.'

'Who are the three?' he asked.

'Maddy, Tom and me, but we thought Andy could be interested, if he is not playing bowls.'

There were no bowls matches that week, and Andy was able to accompany them; so then there were four. Ryta and Maddy had made duck masks on sticks and were wearing big placards around their necks that read: Day of the Ducks. They would be chanting the same mantra as they walked along and blew whistles to alert bystanders to their passion.

The protest was about ducks being kept in barns, bred purely for their meat, rather than being free, swimming on ponds.

'Ducks are aquatic birds,' Ryta told Roger. 'They are not used to being cooped up in barns with no access to water. Did you not take your children to the park to feed the ducks? Children love that, the interaction with living creatures.'

Roger pondered and said he was too old to remember.

'What's your name, Methuselah?' Ryta asked.

'Wait until you're as old as me. If I had a tattoo like Tyler, it would have to be my address, my pin number and yes, my name.'

They all laughed.

Ryta, Elsie and Tom were having lunch in the kitchen; the house was otherwise empty. Ryta started to read the red letter she had taken out of the brown envelope. It stated that Elsie owed £275 for goods from Super Cards, and as she hadn't responded to their request for payment, a debt collector would be calling.

'Don't worry, mum, I'll ring them.'

The debt agency told Ryta that they needed proof of Elsie living at her new address. Utility bills would be sufficient, and they advised Elsie to report it to the police as fraud.

Ryta rang the police and explained that her mum had moved and a lady named Louise had now moved in, who, rumoured to be was always in debt and had supposedly bought lots of items from a catalogue and then put the debt down to Elsie.

Ryta wrote to Super Cards, explaining that Elsie was not a criminal and that she hoped they could resolve the problem as she was an honourable old age pensioner.

Ryta placed her hands together in the prayer position at her heart centre and said, 'Velly honourable, Elsie,' in a Chinese accent.

When Elsie had gone home, Ryta returned to the kitchen to find Maddy had just finished a yoga class and was ready for a chat and a cuppa.

'How is the pole dancing going, Maddy?' Ryta asked. 'I went on a belly dancing course once for six classes; that was fun.'

'Yes, I am really enjoying it,' she said. 'It's different to yoga, that's for sure.'

This is a tale from when Ryta lived as a landlady in a public house, before meeting Tom; the Samantha and David story.

One wintry Monday evening, a table for four people was booked at the pub, in the bar next to the roaring log fire. That day Ryta would meet a couple that were to become her good friends. Ryta had cooked their food and they were enjoying the evening with their friends. When Ryta cleared their plates away, she noticed that one of the ladies was fidgeting in her seat and wincing. Ryta asked if she had a bad back, and she confirmed that she had.

'Would you like some healing when you have finished your meal?' Ryta asked.

The lady agreed. David, her husband, asked what is was, so Ryta explained that she was a member of the National Federation of Spiritual Healers, and that she would say a little prayer and place her hands on Samantha. After enjoying his wine, David laughed at Ryta's proposal and said he thought it was rubbish. Ryta smiled serenely and remarked that we all believe what we want to believe.

Samantha and Ryta went upstairs, where Samantha sat on a chair. Ryta mentally said a prayer and placed her hands on Samantha's shoulders. She told Samantha that she as a healer; was used as a channel by God, Jesus, Buddha or Universal Energy.

When they returned downstairs, David asked Samantha how her back felt, and she said the pain had eased. As they were leaving they noticed a poster advertising a clairvoyant evening at the pub. Samantha decided to book an appointment and asked David if he wanted one too. He prevaricated and they left. The following week, David changed his mind and rang up to book an appointment for himself.

The day arrived. There would be seven mediums upstairs sitting at separate tables, each with an appointment every half an hour. Samantha was booked in with a medium named Marnie Fox, and David would be seen straight afterwards.

He came downstairs looking bemused and said he couldn't believe what she had told him. Samantha and Ryta looked at each other, because they both felt that there are no coincidences, and everything in life is planned. David explained that Marnie had told him he was considering closing his office and working from home, but it seemed too problematical for him. She had advised him to take the plunge and said it would work out just fine. David couldn't understand how she was so accurate and knew what was going on in his life.

Nevertheless, he took her advice and was very happy with the outcome.

Samantha and David also chose to go to Ryta's yoga classes after the pub was closed down. These were held on the pub floor in front of the log fire, and at the end of each session it was time for relaxation, so they were covered with a blanket to keep them cosy.

Maddy had taken on Ryta's classes when Ryta started writing.

'Guess what! A strange thing happened at the Friday night yoga class last week.'

'What's that?' Ryta asked.

Maddy used to hold two yoga classes on a Friday, one at 6.30 p.m. and one at 8 p.m. Edwin and Julia were in the 6.30 p.m. class.

'When we come to yoga, there is always a man sitting in the back of the car,' said Edwin. 'He is a spirit person. When we leave, he comes home with us so far and then disappears.'

'What does he look like?' asked Maddy.

'I will draw a sketch of him,' said Edwin.

He drew a foolscap sketch, placed it on a table and left.

Samantha and David arrived for the next class.

Samantha picked up the picture and said, 'That's my dad!' while David went off to the loo.

When David returned, she asked, 'Who is that, David?'

'Your dad!' he replied.

'Did you draw that, Maddy?' Samantha asked.

'No, Edwin did,' she answered.

'How does Edwin know what my dad looks like?' Samantha enquired.

'He said that the man in the drawing sits in the back of his car on the way to yoga and halfway home, and then disappears. Perhaps he returns to the class because you, David and Peter are all present.' Peter was Samantha's brother.

Samantha agreed that this was probably the case.

When Peter arrived later, she asked him, 'Who was the figure in the sketch?'

'Dad,' he answered.

She then explained how the drawing had come to be on the table.

Truth is stranger than fiction; that is why biographies are often as interesting as fiction, if not more so. Lots of folk have interesting lives, but most don't put pen to paper and write about them.

~

Another Sunday, another tale to be told!

Ryta and Maddy both believed in reincarnation, so Maddy started telling the disbelievers around the table about the picture that one of her pupils had drawn of the spirit person that sat in the back of their car every week. She had previously told this story to Ryta, but Ryta had her own true story to tell from the past, when she previously managed a pub.

On a Sunday evening, a week before the pub closed, three young men and a young woman came in, all in different attire.

One wore a suit and looked like an estate agent, with shiny shoes and his short, dark hair carefully styled. The second was tall and slim with long blonde hair streaming down his back to his waist; definitely a free spirit. The third was good looking and tanned, with dark, curly hair, and wore well-made leather trousers and a leather jacket; a biker, Ryta presumed.

His companion was an attractive girl who wore a mini-skirt, displaying her long, endless legs finishing in knee-high boots. Her top half was adorned by a microscopic cotton top held together with a ring of plastic at the front, displaying a generous cleavage. Mick, the landlord, named her Tits & Bum, as she was known from then on.

They stood warming themselves in front of the roaring fire in the inglenook, remarking what a beautiful building it was.

On the wall opposite was a poster advertising a clairvoyant

evening; £10.00 for a thirty-minute reading. The couple booked themselves in for the following evening.

'Are you a biker?' Ryta asked.

'Yes, I'm like metal Micky. I've fallen off so many times doing wheelies I'm put together with metal plates,' he replied, laughing.

'Do you suffer with many aches and pains?' she asked.

'Yes, wrists and shoulders are the worst, but I don't believe in taking anti-inflammatories.'

'Have you heard about Bioflow magnetic wristbands? They use your body's own self-healing mechanism.'

'How do they work?' he enquired.

'We don't really know, but if you are not happy after a three-month trial period, we are willing to give you a refund, less 15 per cent.'

He thought it sounded like an interesting proposition and took a leaflet.

They duly appeared the next evening and enjoyed being surrounded by likeminded folk waiting, like them, for readings.

It was a friendly, chatty, welcoming establishment, with complete strangers feeling at ease and able to chat to others about the findings of the mediums they had consulted.

During the evening, when chatting to a couple of ladies waiting at the bar, Ryta discovered that they both worked for the local planning department.

She moved to serve two men she hadn't seen for a while.

'Have you got change of use for this pub then?' one asked her.

'No, we can't get permission from the planning department,' she answered.

'Don't you have enough money to go in the brown envelope?' he replied.

'We haven't any spare money to put in any envelope,' was her dismal answer.

At this point the two ladies left the bar area and sat down at a table, out of earshot.

'They both work in the planning department,' Ryta whispered.

'I don't care, everyone knows it goes on,' he said. 'Probably why they walked away.'

Digby returned a few days later to purchase a Bioflow and decided to join as a distributor at the same time. He was back a week later for more stock, after having excellent results with his own. More good reports gave him more sales at the factory where he worked. Digby often phoned to confirm that Ryta was at home before he visited, often with Tits & Bum. In retrospect, it was probably to make sure she got the homemade cake out and put the kettle on!

One day, as Ryta was making tea behind the bar, she received clairvoyance that Digby had a ring in his winky.

She poured the tea and then asked, 'Digby, do you have a ring in your willy?'

Tits & Bum looked sideways at her, and Digby blushed.

'I haven't seen it, honest, I just got it clairvoyantly,' Ryta said to Tits & Bum.

Digby said, 'I have eight pieces of ironmongery in it.'

'Oh!' Ryta replied, with visions of them all jingling and jangling, wondering why she hadn't heard the cacophony before.

'Does it give you greater sexual pleasure?' she asked, realising that she had led a very sheltered sexual existence.

'Yes!' Digby answered with finality.

That was clearly the end of the matter, with no more questions to be asked.

Digby came and went in Ryta's life. A very cosmopolitan soul, he sometimes lived in Portugal, sometimes Canada, but his job in the plastics factory remained open for when he returned from his travels. He was an alive, energetic daredevil of a man, surrounded by friends of all ages and nationalities.

One day, a visitor asked if Ryta had heard about Digby's accident and that he was in hospital.

Ryta quickly phoned his mum. He'd been paragliding behind a car when the wind dropped and he had smashed into the ground. He was rushed to intensive care, where they opened him up, but he was beyond repair and within days he had died.

None of us could believe how someone that vibrant could possibly be dead at the age of thirty-three.

He died on the Friday, and on the Monday three mediums, Ryta and another friend of his met to see if he would contact them to give some evidence of life after death.

Brian was able to communicate and said a man wearing black leathers and doing wheelies on a motorbike was showing himself to him. He said he was sorry for all the grief he was causing as a result of his stupidity.

The day of the funeral was fine and warm. He was being buried at the huge church in Eaton Socon, which was overflowing with his relatives and friends who had flown from all over the world. He had been befriended and loved wherever he went.

The first car contained the coffin, the second his family, followed by a cortège of forty leather-clad motorcycle enthusiasts riding their motorbikes – members of the motorbike club to which he had belonged.

It was cool and calm in the church, the service brief. Most of the congregation then wandered through the sunny churchyard and down the road to quench their thirst at the local hostelry, sitting outside by the river.

This was a celebration of his life, not his death. He enjoyed life to the full, and although it was cut short, he put more into that life than most people did who were three times his age.

Chapter 9
Stories from a Previous Life

'That was really interesting, Ryta. Any more treasured tales from a bygone life?' Roger drawled.

'Well, Roger, since you have been a millionaire, would you like to hear a story about one?'

'Perhaps the story will give me some lessons on how to hang on to it next time,' he replied.

'He did have two helicopters,' Ryta said.

'Sounds like a serious millionaire to me,' Roger replied.

Bill used to come into the pub for a half pint; he was a northern chap, didn't say much, just sat and supped in silence.

When Ryta and Mick first took over the pub, Mick continued working. Ryta tried to build up the pub trade by spending time chatting with the customers.

Bill had polio as a child; he wore a built-up boot and limped. He was, as Ryta gradually learned, a taciturn man. Over the years, he relaxed, disclosing a few details about his life. A very strong character, he wasn't going to let a disability cramp his style, and began his roof tiling business with great success. With the profits he began to purchase terraced houses in Newcastle and found renting them out to be a very lucrative market.

There was talk of a lady in his life, and one day Marlene came into the pub with him. Stunning, slim and blonde, he certainly knew how to pick them! Although reputedly being a millionaire may have been a contributory factor. Eventually, she moved in, they married and had two lovely children, John and Janet.

They seemed happy, although no one knows what goes on behind closed doors. Sadly Bill was a workaholic, and this began to put pressure on their marriage.

Janet, Bill's daughter, decided to find herself a job, so Ryta asked her to do the hoovering at the pub. She was very thorough, a model employee.

One day Ryta noticed a packet of cigarettes was missing from the shelf.

Every evening when the pub closed, the till was balanced and the cigarettes were counted, before being refilled ready for the next day's trading.

That morning there were only two people in the pub, and she knew Janet must have taken the cigarettes. She went to feel in the pockets of her coat hanging on the hooks outside the ladies' toilets. One pocket contained the packet of cigarettes.

Ryta put the coffee machine on and called out to Janet to join her in the garden for their coffee break.

'Do you smoke, Janet?' she asked.

'No,' Janet replied.

Ryta didn't see the point in mincing her words.

'So why have you stolen a packet of cigarettes from me?'

Janet blushed scarlet.

'I've stolen them for the girls at school.'

'Why?'

'They are bullying me and said I had to take them.'

'Well, I shall have to tell your dad,' Ryta said finally.

'No, no don't tell him, he'll kill me,' she begged, and began to cry.

'I'll tell your mum what's going on, then.'

'No, she'll tell my dad, she tells him everything.'

Her crying turned to sobs. Ryta couldn't believe this tall girl was being bullied.

'Why don't you refuse them?'

'They'll get me,' she said, obviously very frightened.

'Your dad would never have allowed himself to be bullied; what do you think he would have done?'

'Punched them, probably.'

'If it comes to that, you must do the same. You must stand up for yourself, Janet; be bold, be brave, have no fear!' Hating to see anyone so distressed, Ryta added, 'Okay, I won't tell anyone if you promise not to steal from me again.'

Janet gave her word and there were no more discrepancies.

~

Ryta used to organise monthly clairvoyant evenings upstairs at the pub and to her surprise, one month Bill booked an appointment. There were seven mediums with a customer booked every half hour, so Ryta was kept busy running up and down the stairs with a clipboard to keep track of the appointments.

Bill duly arrived for his appointment and went upstairs. The half an hour went quickly and he returned to the bar.

'Give me a drink, Ryta, I need one after that.'

Ryta was not surprised.

'She told me I was brought up by my grandparents, which is true, but nobody in this area knew. Also, she said my grandfather was there with her, and she described his appearance accurately. Said he was telling her about his time in the army, in the First World War. She also said that he told her he had been shot in the right shoulder and never regained full use of his arm, and how it just hung loosely. This is all true, but how could she have known?'

'Because she's a medium,' Ryta replied.

Soon after, Bill began to suffer from stress and didn't even want to get up for work, which was unlike him. He just stayed in bed, with no incentive to do anything.

Ryta suggested he spend more time with his family and go on a holiday together, but it was too little, too late.

Marlene, like lots of wives that are work widows, decided that she would like a life. The fact that Ryta was going through a divorce perhaps encouraged her to consider it, although she never mentioned it and kept her thoughts to herself. She frequently called in for a floater coffee, and to ask questions regarding Ryta's progress. Ryta felt she was about to take that step, so was not surprised when she finally did, having heard it through the grapevine.

The moral of this tale is all that glitters is not gold.

~

Another Sunday, Roger said he had been drag hunting. Maddy said, 'You are despicable chasing a live animal. I don't believe it. If there is any justice in the world next time you would come back as a fox and be chased, so you would know what it feels like. They are sentient beings with feelings just like you and me.'

'No, Maddy, they are only animals, to be used for our convenience.'

'You are so wrong, Roger. Have you no compassion for living creatures?'

Ryta redirected the conversation to Andy, a van driver.

'How is your job going, Andy?'

'I'm getting a bit fed up actually and I'd like a change I think, but I don't know what.'

'Perhaps something will come up. How is your daughter Kate?'

'She is doing very well at school,' he said, and produced a photo.

'What a pretty girl; blonde like you, too!' said Ryta.

Andy had had a relationship with a married woman, Marie, fourteen years earlier, and their union produced Kate. Andy couldn't afford the expense of a wife, home and child on his meagre wages, so the husband had agreed to raise the child as part of the family.

The adulterous relationship continued, with Andy taking Marie out whenever he could afford to.

Chapter 10
A Day Out for Elsie

Ryta, Tom and Elsie had travelled to Northampton to the Green Festival. The numerous stalls included the Green Party, Friends of the Earth, the Soil Association, Animal Aid, VIVA (Vegetarian International Voice for Animals), Amnesty International and Greenpeace. Ryta stopped to buy some notelets from the Green Party stall.

'If there was a candidate in Raunds, I'd vote Green,' she said to the lady on the stall.

'Why don't you stand yourself?'

'I don't know about your policies and ideals.'

'You could go to a Green Party meeting to see if it interests you.'

'Okay,' Ryta said. 'When is the next meeting?'

'Tomorrow Monday, in Northampton at 8 p.m.'

'Okay,' she said.

Looking in her diary, she was free, so she agreed to go.

The meeting was at a pub, and ten members were present. The same night Ryta attended, there was also another new lady named Jac. Marcus was the chairman and Jonathan the deputy. The outcome of the meeting was that Jac and Ryta both decided to stand in their respective districts. Both said they did not want to go door knocking, but they did deliver some flyers by hand to remind people of the Green Party values.

They agreed to stand in their localities; the others told them that this was a token gesture and they wouldn't get in, and this echoed in Ryta's ears.

Jonathan helped her fill in all the forms and then took her to meet several councillors at a Parish and Town Councillors' meeting in Thrapston.

The day dawned and Ryta didn't stand outside wearing a rosette and a smile, as she decided that nobody knew who she was; she was an anonymous housewife, unknown, and felt the general public would say, 'Ryta? Ryta who?'

So, safe in the knowledge that she would collect only two votes, hers and Tom's, she sauntered into the counting department.

A young lady approached her with a smile and said, 'Congratulations, Councillor Lyndley.'

'Goodness, there must be some mistake!'

'No, you have received 168 votes and are now the Green Councillor for Raunds.'

'But nobody knows who I am; it must be a protest vote.'

'Congratulations and well done!' said Michelle, the Lady Mayor.

What a shock to the system.

Twice monthly after that, Ryta attended the Council and Environmental Committee meetings to observe, as this was all totally new to her. One week, some well-known building developers were invited to attend. They wanted to request permission to build 160 houses, then more to increase their total to 800. The council did not welcome this request.

Ryta enquired as to whether these properties would be fitted with solar panels and water recycling systems.

'No!' said the developers.

They looked surprised by her question.

'But isn't government legislation encouraging us to include all these measures for energy conservation?' she asked.

Apparently, energy saving and conservation were not high on their agendas, and it was all being done in the name of profit, yet again.

'The government should make all these energy saving ideas a necessity, not just a suggestion, otherwise reducing emissions will never be achieved. If global warming continues, with seas rising as predicted in Norfolk and Suffolk, we will be going on holiday to Cambridge-on-Sea.'

Ryta kept her interest in Bioflow magnetic bracelets because she liked to help folk that were in pain. One day she had a phone call.

'Hello, can I help you?' she answered.

'Are you Ryta, the lady who sells the magnetic bracelets?'

'Yes, that's right.'

'Well, we've been in Higham Ferrers. Where are you now?'

'Raunds.'

'We've been looking for you, Ryta. We're near the Co-Op. Can we walk from here?'

Ryta assumed they meant the Co-Op in Raunds and directed them past the post office on the right, towards the market place.

'The post office is on a side street.'

'No, it's on the main road,' said Ryta.

Ryta continued to give directions into Brick Kiln Road, then Mallows Drive, but clearly both parties had their wires crossed.

'I'll stand in the road and wave my arms. What colour car have you got?'

'Black!'

'Okay, see you in a minute.'

Ryta went outside and started waving her arms at any black car that passed; lots of passengers waved back, but not the Bioflow customers.

A blue sports car drove past, then round the horseshoe before turning back to Ryta.

Two young mums asked, 'Are you okay? Have you broken down?'

'No, I am expecting visitors in a black car. They are having difficulty finding Mallows Drive, so I said I would stand and wave at all the black cars, but thank you for your trouble.'

They drove off. Nice, helpful ladies.

Ryta walked back inside the house. They should have been here by now.

Then a black car appeared.

'Do come in!' Ryta said as they walked up the driveway. They had had quite an adventure. They had been told they could buy a Bioflow bracelet in Higham Ferrers, but the shop had changed hands so they enquired in another shop.

A young man said, 'Do you must mean Ryta? This is her phone number.'

They walked along the High Street and enquired in a beauty salon.

A waiting customer said, 'I bought mine from Ryta.'

They thought everybody in Higham Ferrers must have bought their Bioflows from Ryta. They left the shop to enquire where Brick Kiln Road and Mallows Drive were.

A lady passing by said, 'Follow me, I'll take you there.'

They did, amazed by people's kindness.

This is the balloon story.

After they purchased their Bioflows, they talked about life after death and strange coincidences, deciding that there are no coincidences and everything is planned, but that we do have personal choice. The lady told them a strange story. It was her husband's 60th birthday party, but he was not a party person and didn't really want to have a big do, so it was just going to be a small family affair; his brother had died aged fifty-nine the year before.

The wife purchased some balloons, all different colours and shapes. When everyone was leaving, each child was invited to choose a balloon, until the last guest departed when there were two star-shaped balloons left, one blue, the other one red.

Bill lay on the settee for his afternoon nap and was soon snoring gently. June sat down in the armchair, pleased that the party had been successful.

She stood up to go into the kitchen, and on her return could only see the blue balloon.

That's strange, she thought. Where is the red balloon?

Suddenly, it popped up from behind the armchair and

floated towards the ceiling. She watched as it then drifted along to the archway that divided the two rooms, bobbed under the arch and continued its progress. It circled the room, bobbed under the arch again, then returned and hung suspended from the ceiling.

After a while, Bill woke up and June recounted what had happened.

He said, 'You must have imagined it.'

Whilst they were talking, the balloon set off again on a repeat journey, and they both followed it at a distance. It left the room, turned the corner to the base of the stairs and began its ascent.

When the balloon arrived on the landing, it went into the master bedroom and circled round, watched by the couple from the doorway. As it came slowly back out again, they hurried down the stairs before it. Bill stood at the bottom, and as the balloon went past him, it stopped and rested against his heart. Then it moved back into the adjoining rooms and up to just below the ceiling.

'Isn't that a strange story?' June said.

'No, his brother was just showing him that he's still around, and then by touching his heart he's saying, "I am coming to you with love, as I did when we were together."'

Neither had felt afraid or uncomfortable in any way.

The story reminded Ryta of another funny tale.

Chapter 11
Retired Neighbours

Irene and Charles were neighbours for a number of years until they retired to a bungalow in Bournemouth. After a long illness, Charles died. When Ryta went to visit Irene, she walked into their lounge and asked Irene if she could smell or see cigarette smoke rising to the ceiling from the armchair where he used to sit. He had always been a smoker.

She replied, 'Yes, and sometimes there is a row of cigarette smoke rings drifting slowly upwards.'

She felt him with her, and when she had a difficult job to do, such as putting up curtain rails or something practical, she always asked for his help and felt that she received guidance from him.

~

On another Sunday, the topic of the Colonel's vegetables was brought up.

'What about a stall at the farmers' market?' Maddy suggested.

'Just open a little shop,' Roger suggested.

'The problem with that idea is that there would be overheads, like business tax, rent, staff wages, insurance, water and heating.'

'What a nightmare for the Colonel,' Tom said.

'I actually don't want to be bothered with all that red tape at my age. I am enjoying a stress-free life and want it to continue.'

'Good for you, Colonel; I think the farmers' market is a good idea. And what about giving all the proceeds to charity? Then you won't be getting involved in a business,' Maddy interjected.

'Maddy, you are just a lentil loony. You can't give money away.'

'Why not? We should only have enough for our needs, not our wants, and if it makes the Colonel happy, so be it,' she retorted.

'All this information is giving me a lot to consider when I'm toiling in the garden,' said the Colonel.

~

Ryta went to see Lyn to deliver a couple of Bioflows, as she was a distributor. While she was there, she was asked to give some Reiki healing to Lyn's cat named Florence who was feeling poorly. Then, Ryta went to see a male friend who had circulatory problems.

'Sorry I'm late I was giving Reiki healing to a cat.'

'I hope you washed your hands before touching me,' he said.

'No!' she replied, and hooted with laughter.

'I might catch something; those cats have fleas.'

'I loved my dog so much I used to bite his neck and ear; and he was very appreciative and groaned with pleasure.'

'Oh no! Not all those germs!'

'I think my dog had less germs than most people. Think of all those folks who have AIDS.'

'What about your dog's teeth? They weren't cleaned like a human's.'

'Oh yes they were! I used to brush them with Eucryl Smokers' powder and I got him out of the bad habit of smoking! Ha, ha ha!' Ryta convulsed with laughter at this exchange.

He had always been an alcoholic and was not keen on exercising, and eventually, as his circulation became more sluggish, his skin thinned and his legs became ulcerated. His doctor advised him that he was drinking himself to death, but addicts only believe what they want to believe. This led to him becoming housebound and his legs had to be dressed by a health visitor, but still he drank. The weeping sores got bigger and he was unable to climb the stairs to bed, but still he drank, sleeping in his armchair. Incontinence came next as his organs were gradually destroyed.

When Ryta visited he would ask how she seemed so young and vibrant, and she would reply truthfully that it was because she was not an alcoholic.

'I'm not either,' he would say, and she would point to the empty bottles under his chair.

He would explain that they were from yesterday, but alcoholics always have an excuse.

One day when Ryta was visiting, he was reminiscing about when they were young lovers.

'You had the most beautiful breasts, Ryta. Would you show them to me one more time?'

She didn't hesitate and stood up, whisked off her top and bra, and said, 'Happy now?'

He laughed and said, 'I won't get treats like this in hospital. I'm going in on Friday.'

Two weeks later, Ryta visited him in a small ward in Bedford Hospital.

'What ward is this?' she asked.

'The death ward, when we go to sleep at night there are six in bed, but there is always an empty bed in the morning.'

'Are your legs any better?'

'Just the same,' he replied, never one to moan.

When it was time to say goodbye, she kissed his cheek as he held her hand.

'We had some good times together, Ryta, didn't we?'

'Yes, we did,' she replied, and they both knew this was their final goodbye.

He died the next day in his hospital bed.

~

Ryta returned to find the Colonel toiling in the garden again.

'Tea, Colonel?'

'Yes, please!'

'How old is your dog Omo?'

'He'll be ten soon.'

'Quite a good age, then.'

'Well, they can live to be twenty, if I'm lucky. I expect he'll see me out.'

'Now, now, don't be depressing. You could live to be a hundred if you wanted to, what with your interest in Omo and gardening, not to mention the stall at the farmers' market, or wherever else your plans take you.'

'Yes, I am still debating the pros and cons of that idea.'

'Perhaps we could set up a rota for the stall. What about two volunteers in the morning and two in the afternoon? Then it wouldn't be so arduous for you. What do you think? You could even take Omo to attract the children to come over.'

'That's a good idea!' He smiled, as he did whenever he talked or thought about Omo, his best friend.

Ryta could relate to the Colonel's affection for his dog; her own dog Zeus was now deceased, and had left a hole in her life. This had been her life before number 41, when she was married to Mick and lived in the pub.

Chapter 12
Beloved Pet, Zeus

Zeus was given to Ryta and Mick when they lived at Ye Olde Plough Public House, as he was too tall at the shoulder to take part in dog shows. A lady named Valerie who bred Dobermans just wanted to be sure he had a good home and was loved. They were lucky to meet her requirements.

Zeus settled in with their cats Chubby, Titchy Woo and Blacky Boo. They curbed his boisterous nature with a look or hiss, as they knew that within that six stone of muscle was a warm heart that contained no malice.

Titchy Woo defended him one day when a tiny, yappy dog was bouncing up and down, trying to reach up and snap at his nose. Poor Zeus found this disconcerting, as he thought everyone loved him, and to discover this was not the case and to be on the receiving end of such hostility was quite a shock. He stood looking puzzled, and then Titchy Woo decided to intervene.

He sprang between the two dogs, raised his fur and hissed.

'Stop harassing my friend, or you'll be on the end of my claws!'

The small, yappy dog retreated sheepishly to his mistress and the crisis was over!

One winter's day, after the snow had fallen, a delivery arrived. Ryta was checking it off when Zeus spotted a rabbit through the open front door and ran off in hot pursuit. She and Mick went looking for him, but he was long gone. Then they had a phone call from a neighbour.

'I think your dog is in my garden. But because he is so big, I don't want to approach him,' she said.

Ryta and Mick drove to the house and saw Zeus in the front garden.

'Hello, Zeus,' Ryta said.

He stood up and then sat down again on his two broken back legs, having been hit by a car. The driver was unable to stop the car in the snow as the doggy whirlwind swept in front of it.

The poor man came over and apologised, knowing how upset folk are when their loved ones are hurt. They took him to the vets, and they phoned Cambridge Veterinary College to arrange for him to be operated on immediately. He had a collapsed lung and was in shock, so the two broken legs would have to wait until his body and breathing had stabilised.

He was there for ten days and they were not allowed to visit, as it would have destabilised his delicate condition. When his lungs were working again, his legs were operated on and he was returned to them in plaster casts.

The customers loved petting the ailing dog, and he loved the fuss. He lay in the big leather armchair in front of the fire to accept the adulation, which he felt was his right!

When the plasters were removed, emerald-green bandages adorned his back legs. Eventually, he returned to good health, although remained slightly arthritic. But he wore a Bioflow magnetic collar and was always mobile.

He was a lovely dog, more human than animal; he knew what you were thinking to the extent that when the dog nail clippers were produced, he was off the couch like a rocket and orbiting the room at warp speed!

There were days when he was calm and relaxed, and he participated in Ryta's yoga class by listening to the philosophy being read out, while drifting in and out of sleep on the settee in the alcove called the Cuddling Corner.

When stroking Zeus, Mick noticed a wound five inches in diameter on his chest. They hadn't noticed it before, because he had always been lying on that side. Sandra the vet was one of Ryta's yoga pupils, so after the class, whilst the other pupils were enjoying their coffee, Sandra examined Zeus.

'This is not good news, Ryta,' she remarked sadly. 'It is a cancerous growth; you can see all his intestines.'

Ryta accepted the diagnosis, as she approached everything in life philosophically.

'Well, all I can do is pray and give him Reiki healing,' she said.

The class departed gloomily after hearing the news, as they all loved Zeus' exuberance, and how he eyed up the biscuits or cake on the table after class.

'Okay, Zeus, I'm going to give you healing to try to make you a well dog.'

He knew exactly what Ryta was saying, and turned his huge head round, looked her in the eye and placed his nose on her cheek. He never licked people he wasn't that sort of dog.

The Reiki healing continued on a daily basis until the wound shrank to a scab the size of a tiny fingernail, an inch long.

The pupils asked Sandra why she hadn't been able to help Zeus, as they knew she was a vet and had studied for seven years. Ryta was just a yoga teacher, yet he had recovered. Sandra explained that Ryta was a channel for God, Jesus, Buddha and Universal Energy, and whatever your beliefs, sometimes healing worked and sometimes it didn't, but it had worked on Zeus.

He lived for another two years, to be one month short of twelve years old, which is a good age for a Doberman. He died peacefully in his sleep with only a few grey hairs on his muzzle. Perhaps the cancer was the result of the life-threatening accident, which had led to the collapsed lung and broken legs.

The Colonel had listened with quiet interest and said, 'Yes, they are sadly missed.'

'But you can only give them a good home and love them whilst they are here, just like husbands.'

The Colonel laughed at her comparison.

'Never had a wife myself, too busy with the army. But there is still time. I might find myself a jolly filly; never too old. Charlie Chaplin was still fathering children at eighty!'

They both laughed.

Ryta said, 'Well, if you use it, you don't lose it. Remember that, Colonel. Te he!'

Chapter 13
Roger, the Dodger

Another week, another Sunday, and this time it was Roger's 50th birthday, so there was wine on the table again. He was very open-handed, always first at the bar to buy a round of drinks, so was popular at the local pub, the Axe and Compass.

He would walk in and say, 'Let me buy everyone a drink,' to Beatrice, the landlady, who happily obliged.

His sense of humour was legendary, more insulting than complimentary, but it was just his way.

He would comment to the landlord, Jason, 'When are you going to get rid of this dozy barmaid? She is so slow,' talking about the landlady.

She fell about with laughter, enjoying such humour, which was just as well.

If he met a local with his wife or regular girlfriend, he would say, 'When are you going to get rid of this ugly bird and get yourself a decent woman?'

You had to be thick-skinned when Roger was around.

After the birthday lunch everyone sang Happy Birthday. Then, after more than a few glasses of wine, Roger began to open up, as he felt they were all becoming like family, and his colourful story of earlier years was told.

He had married too young, and the unfortunate shotgun marriage resulted in an unfeeling, insensitive son, who was bought up with a public school education. He later became a member of a shooting group that perhaps did not value and treat animals as kindly as they should have done. They used to go hare coursing, roaring across the fields in a Land Rover at night, switching on the lights and shooting as many hares and rabbits as possible.

The odd cat that got in the way was treated like a rat, being shot like vermin. There was no consideration for the pet or the bereaved owner. Perhaps this was in part due to his loveless relationship with his father.

Roger felt the burden of having a son had led to this inconvenient marriage. We don't always accept that situations are usually of our own making, but Roger had become more philosophical with hindsight and age.

His next relationship was with Prisalla, a high-flyer in the jewellery business. Their relationship led to a daughter, Sandy. Roger felt that he could not commit after one failed marriage, so they parted, Prisalla taking Sandy with her.

Prisalla went on to meet a good-looking farmer, younger than herself, willing to give her marriage, stability and twin daughters. She used her business acumen to change his farming losses into a thriving equestrian centre; she had finally met her Prince Charming.

Roger had been a millionaire twice, but lost it all in bad business deals; the second time was on Black Thursday, when the stock markets crashed and he lost his punters a lot of money. Still ever the optimist, Roger was now looking to make his third million.

'Wouldn't you rather have done it once and hung onto it?' Ryta asked.

'It's the fun of it; living on a knife's edge keeps the adrenalin going,' he replied with a wink, shrugging his shoulders and singing Money, Money, Money by Abba.

While they were all relaxing, Maddy mentioned an old acquaintance to Ryta.

Roger, ever on the lookout for female company, said, 'What does she look like?'

'Ugly,' said Maddy.

There was stunned silence.

'That was a conversation stopper, Maddy,' said Andy.

'Well, I think if somebody is ugly on the inside, it shows in their face.'

Slowly Ryta ventured, 'Maybe you could be right! If she had

had a relationship with that builder, Greg, it might have done her the world of good.'

'What was that about?' Roger asked, intrigued by the conversation.

'He did all this work for her and she didn't want to pay him,' Maddy explained. 'Oh yes, and he told her that he'd been in love with her since she was eighteen when they'd worked together at the Axe and Compass around the corner. She was a student and he was a chef. So she thought she would capitalise on that and he would do all the work for nothing. He tried to coerce her into bed. She refused to pay, despite being happy with the work, so he had to take her to court to get his money.'

Sometimes professional folk like her, now a qualified doctor, feel that builders are not in the same class. It would be sad if her epitaph read 'Returned unopened'.

'How is your gardening career going, Tyler?' Tom asked.

'Fine. These old ladies love to feed and look after me; I think they like the company and the chat over a cup of tea. They ask what I've been doing, if I've got a girlfriend and all about you lot now they know I live in bedsit land.'

'Excuse me,' Ryta interjected. 'These are studio flats, not bedsits. We are upmarket, aren't we?'

'So how did you get in then, Ryta?' Tom dug her in the ribs. 'Especially with your little bit of rough, me!' He laughed.

'When I met Tom, we had a joint Barclaycard and one of the entries was Wilko.'

'What's this Wilko? Is it a builder's merchant?'

'No, Wilkinson's! You've really gone down the drain since you met me.'

They all joined in with the laughter.

Sometimes Elsie was present at the lunch. She was popular with the guests, probably because she had a habit of calling a spade a spade. She was recounting her visit to the new Waitrose.

'Posh shop,' she said. 'The assistant asked if I would like cash back. I said, "Why? I've just paid." She explained that I could have cash back from my card and I asked her where it came from. "Off your bank card," she said. I asked her what she meant, and she said, "It comes out of your bank account." I said thank you, but no!'

Andy had a new girlfriend called Cindy. They'd met down the local pub, the Axe and Compass. He was still friends with Marie, Kate's mum, and was appreciative of the love, care and understanding that Kate was given, as she had a hearing defect, which made school rather difficult.

His relationship with Cindy went from strength to strength. He changed his job to work at the local recycling plant with an increase in salary, and with Cindy's wage they decided to set up home together.

We were all sad when Andy left, but pleased that he had a lady of his own to care for. He came back on a regular basis to chat, eat and catch up on the news.

Tyler moved upstairs into Andy's old room, so Angelina came back to her old room, as Jeff the jeweller had been no more considerate of her feelings than the first time round. She was heartbroken, but a pretty girl like that would not be lonely for long. She did not understand what a devastating effect she had on men. She had an inferiority complex and always thought she was fat. Even when she looked in the mirror, she couldn't see the beautiful woman reflected within it.

Angelina had taken the separation from Jeff hard, having thought he was sincere when he asked her to return and promised to be faithful. She was pouring out her woes to Ryta while the house was empty.

'Unfortunately, some men are serial adulterers and just need to keep proving they are irresistible. Loving one person in their life is not enough. You have given him two shots, but a leopard doesn't change its spots. Have you thought about a holiday or a change of scenery?' Ryta said.

'Funny you should say that. I do have an Aunty Barbara who lives in Brittany; she is always asking me to go and stay, so perhaps I will take her up on her offer.'

'The Eurostar is a lovely smooth ride,' Ryta said. 'Better than some of the rides you've been having lately!'

Chapter 14
Barbara's Bonanza

Barbara and Dirk were married with two beautiful children, Kelly and Thomas. They were the perfect family; two beautiful people with perfect children.

The fairy tale didn't end there. Dirk, a builder, was slim, unremarkable and unassuming, and a serial adulterer. Barbara forgave him time and time again. She was a strong woman who always managed to earn her own money, but he had one affair too many and she asked him for a divorce.

Dirk was shocked, and yet again promised he would be faithful, but for Barbara this time there were to be no second chances.

The children were adults now. Kelly was soon to be wed, and Thomas was good with his hands and worked as a car mechanic. So for Barbara, there was no compromise. The old manor house, with its original beams and unusual pargetting, had to be sold. Kelly was wed, and a united front was presented to friends and relatives before the split.

Barbara dropped a bombshell when she announced she had decided to go and live in Brittany. Her friends knew she liked to holiday there, but to go there to live was another ball game! Barbara, not one to feel daunted, explained that in her younger days she had been a student in France and had lived there for two years. She had enjoyed the experience, so this mid-life crisis had led her to focus on searching for a more relaxed lifestyle.

After several visits she eventually secured a gîte, which included three quarters of an acre of land and a run-down barn. She thought it was a snip at the price, and was contemplating her new life with anticipation, expectation and exhilaration.

She had remained friends with her ex-husband, and both he and her son helped her with the move. Once settled in, she joined the local Boules club, mostly consisting of pensioners and singles over fifty. A sociable butterfly and communicator, she was soon offering a helping hand to her elderly neighbours, and her French came up to speed.

Romance was on the cards when Barbara went to a barn dance with friends. She had been blessed with striking looks, so was quickly propositioned by a local Frenchman called Jean-Claude. He had a wife, but in France this was an unimportant detail; he now had a mistress too. This situation was handled discreetly, which suited both parties for a while, but Barbara began to feel sensitive about the situation and wanted more of a commitment.

English builders had started to infiltrate Brittany at this time, so John decided to purchase some dilapidated properties for renovation. It was a meeting of minds and bodies, and Barbara could see that with her barn and gîte completed, there were good prospects of getting tenants.

Her English friends soon beat a path to her door to enjoy her home, her company and the excellent food always available in France.

Angelina needed a break, and it seemed an ideal opportunity. Barbara met her at the train station and she quickly settled into her holiday home.

First stop was the Boules club, where the members were eager to meet another English woman. They had discovered that any friend of Barbara's was usually good fun.

'Parlez-vous le français?' they said to Angelina.

'Un peu, un peu,' Angelina answered.

Barbara explained that Angelina didn't speak much French and only knew a limited number of words that she remembered from her school days.

The locals picked their teams, but Angelina was left until last. This English woman was an unknown quantity; she could be useless and lose the game.

'Merde!'

The first game commenced. Angelina had trouble aiming the ball by the Jack, and her team's faces showed their growing frustration.

Game two, and she was away. They won, so it was neck and neck. Game three, and she played the winning throw. The team danced with joy and, in typical French manner, began embracing each other.

'Très bon, très bon!'

Angelina, emboldened by their praise, suddenly remembered a phrase.

'Henri, voulez-vous une promenade avec moi ce soir, s'il vous plaît?' She fluttered her long eyelashes.

'Oui, oui!' he answered.

Both teams laughed at this sudden inspiration on Angelina's part, poking Henri in the ribs in jocular fashion. Then they all sat down to the inevitable glass of wine always provided after the games.

Angelina had a lovely time with her Aunty Barbara and decided to stay for a further six months to see if she liked the French way of life.

The next time Andy came to visit, it was with Cindy and to tell us the good news that they were engaged. With another celebratory occasion, this was becoming a cosy home for drop-ins and dropouts, but it was Christmas, and every year Ryta boxed up ten shoeboxes for the orphans and refugees.

The charity is named Christmas Child, and at Christmas time over a million boxes are collected and delivered to children worldwide, some of whom will never have received a present before in their lives. Some of the children are filmed receiving their Christmas boxes, and the delight and wonder on those small faces has to be seen.

We have everything we could possibly want in this country, with riches aplenty and more than enough to spare. Water in the tap, food in the cupboards a roof over our heads, heating, and if you have someone to love and who loves you (even if it's your cat), what else do you need?

The first year after giving, Ryta received a newsletter with a photo of a man holding out a box to a child in a shelter reminiscent of a cardboard shack; some actually live in old railway carriages.

This child didn't take the box from the man, so he asked her mother, 'Does she not know what a present is? Is that why she won't accept it?'

Her mother replied, 'No, it's because she has no arms.'

A box is provided to give untold pleasure, not least because gypsy children are not allowed to go to school unless they pay for their own pens, pencils and notepads. These items are given to allow them an education, which otherwise would be denied.

Elsie also gave gifts to the Christmas boxes for children. When she was shopping, if she noticed a bargain, such as woolly hats for children for 50p, she would buy ten.

One day, Ryta visited Elsie to see if she wanted to go out.

'I never know what I am doing from one day to the next with you,' said Elsie.

They were driving along and Ryta was talking to her mum, who was sitting in the back seat, but received no response.

'Tom, can you tell my mum what I just said?'

Tom turned to Elsie, repeating the words.

Elsie saw his mouth move, and then said, 'I can't hear what you're saying. I didn't have time to put my hearing aids in.'

Tom and I laughed about one who can't walk (Tom) and one who can't hear (mum), although not intentionally mocking the afflicted. Laughter is always a welcome tonic, especially if you can laugh at yourself.

Chapter 15
Suzie Wong

There were two rooms at the top of the three-storey house: a large room where Ryta and Tom lived, and another room for a guest, which was now completed. Ryta put out a bed and breakfast sign and soon a lady knocked on the door.

'Hello, I am enquiring if there are any vacancies?'

'Please come in. Would you like to see the room?'

'Yes, please!'

They climbed both flights of stairs and Ryta opened the door to the room.

'Oh, it's lovely!' the lady said as she noted it was clean and cosy, with matching curtains, duvet and complementary decor. Ryta opened the door to the en suite.

'Yes, I am sure it will be fine,' the lady said, and the price was agreed for five nights.

She said she would move her clothes in the next day.

'Are you working in the area?' Ryta asked.

'Yes, I am pharmacist, a locum. I find it interesting to go to different practices, as all doctors seem to operate differently these days.'

'What do you mean?'

'Well, some are considering holistic methods now, instead of filling folks up with pills that often have side effects worse than the illnesses themselves.'

'Yes, people have told me that happens,' Ryta said, nodding her head. 'My mum had sciatica whilst we were on holiday. She was prescribed liquid morphine, which made her really poorly, and her face and ankles swelled up. Then she was given antihistamines to reduce the swelling.'

'What's this then, another lodger, Ryta?' Roger asked with a smile when she went back downstairs.

'Not lodgers, Roger, guests!'

He had noticed that the bed and breakfast sign had quickly disappeared.

'Who have we got coming to join the merry band?' he asked with a wink and a smile. 'Is it a gorgeous, shapely female?'

'She is a Chinese pharmacist who keeps chickens and will be here from Monday to Friday.'

'Oh, Suzie Wong,' he said, visualising a lookalike in a silk Chinese dress.

His imagination working overtime, he started to hum Pretty Woman with a thoughtful look on his face.

The next day, reality kicked in. He walked into the kitchen hoping to confirm his daytime fantasies about the Chinese pharmacist when he saw a rather large lady enjoying a cup of tea with Ryta.

'Oh, Roger! This is Mary-Ann.'

His fantasies disappeared immediately.

'Hello!' he said. 'Any post for me, Ryta?'

Searching through his letters, he disappeared back to his room.

The weekend came around quickly and Mary-Ann had returned to her husband and chickens, so the regulars were enjoying their social Sunday meal.

'What's the pharmacist like, Ryta?' Tyler asked.

'Chinese, married and keeps chickens.'

'Is she dishy?' he asked.

'No, she'd get a part in parade of the porkies, I think,' Roger said.

'Roger! That's not very kind,' Ryta said reprovingly. 'You can't always judge a sausage by its skin.'

'That's probably her problem, too many sausages.'

'All filled with saturated fat,' Maddy chimed in. 'Blocking up her arteries. Do you know insurance companies give cheaper insurance for veggies, as they live longer and are less likely to have heart attacks, cancer or strokes.'

'What's the difference between veggies and vegans,

Maddy?' the Colonel asked. 'I know Ryta is veggie and you are vegan.'

'Veggies eat mainly fruit, vegetables, pulses, rice, eggs and sometimes dairy. Vegans do not eat anything with a face, or anything derivative from animals! It is a plant-based diet. No butter, cheese, eggs, no honey from bees or leather from animals.'

'Goodness, what do you two live on?'

'Lots of good food, that's why I have so much energy,' Ryta replied. 'How many other old age pensioners go swimming, dancing and keep fit weekly, as well as doing daily yoga practice?'

Maddy agreed that Ryta had as much energy as she did at forty purely because of her lifestyle; plus she was happy with her job, relationship and where she lived.

'Despite living with you, Tom.' Ryta poked him as he gave a huge grin.

'I know, you love my assets,' he said.

'That's true!'

'You know I have a twinkle in my winkle!'

Everyone at the table guffawed. They liked the happy, positive couple that always liked to laugh.

'How's your book coming along, Ryta?' the Colonel asked.

'Oh, I write some here and there,' she replied. 'Would you like me to read you a bit? It will be like listening to the radio.'

'The only problem with that is you can't turn the volume down,' Tom interjected.

Mary-Ann enjoyed the Sunday soirées, so she made an effort to arrive back by 6 o'clock, just in time to eat.

'What's it like being a locum, Mary-Ann?' the Colonel asked.

'Very interesting and amusing,' she answered serenely.

'Amusing is probably not a word I would use to describe a pharmacist,' he said.

'I like studying human behaviour from behind my dispensary. How the biggest bag of prescription medicine seems to make the patient feel more important than someone with a small bag. One prescription comes in a small bag, but any more and you receive them in a carrier bag. It's like a badge of honour. I'm more poorly than you are ... I take fifteen tablets a day.'

Maddy leapt in at this point. 'Doctors are not addressing the cause, just masking the symptoms, and they get paid for every prescription they write. They kill folk all the time. I don't mean them personally, but the pharmaceutical companies all in the pursuit of profit.'

Mary-Ann replied, 'Yes, you're quite right of course, but I have a living to earn, to feed my chickens. If people don't want to take personal responsibility for themselves and just take what they are given, that is their choice.'

'Tell me about your chickens,' said the Colonel. 'Why did you decide to keep them?'

'Well, I have a friend whose son has a small animal sanctuary. When battery farms occasionally close, the chickens are found new homes, and I took six of the beauties.'

'Have they all got names?'

'Oh yes, I call them my girls. They are kept in a coop, but at weekends my husband and I take them to our allotment, where we have put up a plastic fence so that they can run free, peck and preen themselves. They love it! In fact, it's difficult to get them back in the carrying box to take them home again. They are quite mischievous and run off, they like it there so much. They all have their own personalities and are all named after good human qualities.'

'What good qualities?' Roger raised his eyebrows.

'Now, Roger, try not to be pessimistic,' Ryta put in. ' What names have you given them, Mary-Ann?'

'Grace, Honour, Patience, Faith, Honesty and Joy, but not when I am chasing them around the allotment!'

They all laughed, visualising Mary-Ann chasing all the naughty chickens.

'The other day, they had a shock. Another gardener had brought his Scottie dog with him, and when he saw my girls he ignored the fence and ran right through it! The fence went up in the air, as did the chickens with lots of squawking. What a commotion!'

They could all visualise such pandemonium and tried to stifle their laughter, but with little success.

Mary-Ann was becoming an amusing addition to the social Sunday set.

'Mrs Brown next door is expecting some chickens tomorrow. I wonder if hers will be ex-battery hens?' Ryta mused.

Mary-Ann said, 'There are now 300,000 homes keeping happy chickens.'

'What price are they to buy?' Roger asked.

'Between £40 and £100 per chicken, depending on the breed.'

'It's a good investment I suppose, with the eggs that you get in return, knowing that the chickens have been fed good grain, with no additives, no chemicals, no growth hormones, and of course the taste of a freshly laid egg is beyond comparison.'

'Well done, Roger; have you been reading my notes?' Maddy asked him mischievously.

A few days later, the Colonel was hoeing in the garden.

Ryta was outside with him, and as she looked over the fence to next door, she said, 'Look, Mr Brown's got his cock out!'

The Colonel looked shocked and then heard loud crowing.

'The hens will be pleased to have a new friend,' Ryta said.

Chapter 16
Maddy is Transported

Maddy decided to buy a new car, but her funds did not allow her to spend more than £200. She started asking everyone she knew if they knew anyone who had a second-hand car for sale, but £200 was the ceiling price. She knew that if you put your request out to the Universe, it rarely fails you. Her yoga pupils were also asked, until Julie said that their dad's car was for sale.

Maddy felt her prayers had been answered.

I'd like to pay for an MOT before I buy it, because I really need to get a year's motoring out of it for £200,' she said.

Julie said, 'Yes, £200 and he will pay for the MOT.'

'Goodness, what a bargain.'

A few weeks went by and not a word regarding the car. Maddy decided to ring Julie's dad.

'Hello Mr Potter it's Maddy here! Is everything okay with the car?'

'Yes, it's just that the man who's doing the MOT has been on holiday, but everything is under control. Would you like a test drive, or to look at it?'

'No thanks it will be fine. If it's good enough for Mrs Potter, it will be good enough for me.'

He was amazed by her faith in him, but said, 'When it's ready I will give you a ring.'

'Okay,' she said.

Maddy picked it up and was very happy to have her own set of wheels.

After about six months the speedometer stopped working, but that was only a minor detail as she always kept to the speed limit, so she just drove everywhere using the rev counter instead. The months went by and the car sailed through its MOT, so the £200 had been well spent. Then disaster struck.

Maddy first had trouble with her car shortly after it was serviced. One week later it wouldn't start on the driveway. The garage took it away and said it needed a new starter motor at a cost of £400.

'That is more than I paid for the car,' she replied indignantly.

'Well, it's that or hit it with a spanner.'

'Is a twelve-inch one big enough?' Maddy asked.

So armed, Maddy drove unremittingly until one day when she came out of the Co-Op with her shopping to find it had given up the ghost!

She had never opened the bonnet before; that was men's work, wasn't it?

She looked around for a suitable male. Next to her was a white van. White van men are friendly, aren't they?

'Excuse me.'

He jumped.

'Could you possibly open my bonnet? I think there is something you touch on the right under the dashboard.'

'Yes, of course.'

Walking round to the front of the car, he said, 'There is usually a catch under here.'

She appeared with her twelve-inch spanner and propped up the bonnet with the support.

'You look professional with that,' he said, eyeing the spanner.

'No; this is the first time I've used it.'

She whacked the starter motor hard and got back in the car; it started first time.

'Well done!' he said admiringly.

She thanked him and drove home.

'The Dalai Lama is coming to England,' Maddy announced one Sunday.

'Who's that?' Roger asked.

'A spiritual person who is head of the Tibetans; like the Pope is the head of Rome. So I shall be going to Nottingham to see him.'

'What does he do, give talks?' the Colonel asked.

'Yes, he travels worldwide to bring peace to the world.'

'Yes, I've heard of him,' Tyler joined in. 'Some of my friends at the commune were Buddhists.'

'So when are you going, Maddy?' Ryta asked.

'Sunday afternoon, so I shall be missing dinner. Boohoo!' She laughed. 'But it will be worth it.'

'Are you driving or going by train?'

'I may drive, but I expect Nottingham town centre will be a nightmare.'

'You can borrow my satnav,' Roger offered.

'Ooh, that sounds complicated, having to look at that as well as negotiate the roads and traffic lights.'

'I could take you if you can stand me; I'm free this Sunday. The countryside from Market Harborough to Nottingham is very picturesque.'

'This is rather sudden, Roger. Are you sure you want to be seen with an ageing lentil loony like me?'

'Well, you have to rough it sometimes.'

She rapped the back of his knuckles with her dessertspoon as a reply.

'Ouch! That's not very loving.'

'Roger, there will be no loving on this trip, watch my lips.'

Ryta then redirected the conversation to other, more neutral topics.

The following Sunday the table guests had changed again, with no Maddy or Roger; they must have reconciled their differences and joined forces after all, albeit temporarily. Ryta and Tom were also missing, having gone away for the weekend to a vegetarian bed and breakfast in Cromer. Elsie was in charge, doing well to cook for the stragglers with a Quorn cottage pie.

The Colonel had heard about her problems with various bodies and Tom's problems with his insurance company.

He mentioned to Elsie that he had a problem of his own and sought her advice.

'Look at this, Elsie. I've been paying this policy for ten years to cover my funeral, but with rising costs I can't afford to continue. Do you think I should let it lapse?'

'Have you any money in an account?'

'Yes.'

'Enough to bury you?'

'Yes, £2,000!'

'Then I should cancel it. Personally I don't believe in insurance. I think it's all a con, trying to get money out of people. Ted, my husband, and I always paid our premiums for years and never claimed, so when he died I decided not to pay again. I do have buildings insurance, but not contents, and certainly not health insurance. I just eat well and exercise in moderation, which I think has helped me to live to this age.'

'Thank you for your advice I'll cancel it; perhaps you can help me compose a letter to explain why I won't be renewing?'

'Yes, I'll do that.'

They sat quietly and began drafting the letter.

Dear Sir,

Thank you for your letter, but unfortunately, being an OAP and still alive in this economic downturn, I do not have the resources to continue to pay your premiums. The heating and food bills must take precedence. When I die I expect I shall be disposed of on the local tip, unless of course there is a considerable charge, but by then these details will be of no concern to me. I do feel that all the payments have been taken under false pretences, because I now cannot afford to continue paying; so ten years' premiums have been wasted.

Yours parsimoniously,

Colonel Henshaw

~

Tom and Ryta were out on the town in Cromer. They walked past the cricket pavilion in the park and saw a marquee erected with loud disco music coming from inside.

'That looks lively,' Ryta said.

'If Giorgio's is quiet tonight, we'll come back here.'

They went upstairs to the boogie bar before the musicians were set up and ready to perform. They joined another couple at a table, started chatting and said they couldn't wait to dance. The band began playing very loudly, and they realised it was heavy rock.

Ryta said to Tom, 'I don't suppose we'll be doing a lot of dancing to that!' The din continued. Suddenly, they heard a tune they recognised and knew it was now or never! They popped up like a couple of elves from behind a toadstool and began strutting their stuff.

The black leather-clad bikers and Hells Angels, their jackets festooned with chains, stood with their huge hands cupped round their pint jugs. They stood in an open-legged stance in their heavy biker boots, looking in disbelief at their audacity.

They were unaware that they were supposed to revere this rock band and just listen. The band stopped, and they smiled and waited.

Ryta said, 'As we're the last ones on the floor, do we get the spot prize?'

There was no answer. They knew the band wouldn't disappoint the regular punters, and when they resumed their playing, the dancers continued too.

One boogie was better than none, so they decided to see if they would be welcome at the cricket pavilion.

On entering the marquee, Tom asked if he could buy two tickets for the disco. The lady said it was a private party, but if they wanted to ask the lady in the blue dress, whose party it was, she was sure she wouldn't mind if they stayed.

They approached the lady, who introduced herself as Maggie and explained the party was in celebration of her 25th wedding anniversary. She said they were both very welcome to help themselves to free champagne and food.

They had a wonderful time dancing to all the old favourites. Then Tom, always hungry, decided to sample the buffet. The table was groaning under the weight of huge platters of thickly sliced ham, pork, beef and turkey, with salmon fillets too.

It was soon time to go, and as Maggie's guests were departing, she was asking them to take home food, wrapped in foil parcels, to minimise the waste.

'Please take what you like, otherwise it will go in the bin,' she said, so Ryta obliged and in return gave her a copy of her book as an exchange of energies.

Chapter 17
A Visit to the Dalai Lama

The following Sunday, the missing four returned.

'Did you two have a good time?' Tom asked.

'Yes, it was an experience,' Roger answered. 'Jonathon Dimbleby was there with three schoolchildren asking the Dalai Lama questions.'

'Questions from the mouths of babes.'

'What were they?'

'One was from a six year old, who asked if the earth was hurting because of the way we are treating it. Another asked what will happen to the world if there are too many people, and I can't remember the third.'

'What answers did he give?'

'He said yes, the earth is hurting, which is why we are experiencing freak weather conditions, and the over-population problem means that more people will have to become nuns and monks. We all laughed at that. He is just like on TV, always happy and smiling.'

'Ah, the third question was whether he thinks the Tibetans will ever return to Tibet,' Maddy remembered, 'and he said yes, one day they will all return. How positive is that?'

'As the Aborigines have been pardoned in Australia, perhaps the Australian prime minister, who is reputedly a friend of the Chinese prime minister, may eventually be able to influence a change of views on Tibet by allowing them all to return to their homeland.'

'Guess what? Maddy is now sponsoring a Tibetan child,' said Roger.

'What does that involve?' said Angelina.

'I've paid £190 to subscribe towards a child's education. Tibetan children are not allowed to pursue their religious beliefs or be educated traditionally, so they are escaping across the Himalayas to India to join the Dalai Lama where he now lives.

Sometimes they suffer from frostbite and lose toes, but they are very courageous. They see how education is contributing to world peace and feel it is of great importance for everyone.'

'Pity the children here don't see things the same way,' the Colonel added.

Maddy answered thoughtfully, 'But the children there have a loving, disciplined upbringing, totally different to the "never say no to children" society we have here, with all the resulting social problems.'

'What do you mean, Maddy?' asked Angelina.

'I feel that if children were to understand the word no, they would be able to use it themselves when offered drugs, drink or cigarettes, which we all know are not good for any of us.'

Tom interrupted. 'The advertising budgets of the big corporations would have to be cut for that to happen. The government could curtail binge drinking if they reduced advertising on TV.'

~

It was another social Sunday, and Andy had come back for some lunch.

'How was your trip to France?' he asked Angelina.

'Really good! My Aunty Barbara is a real live wire, got more energy than me. We played boules and went to a barn dance. It was great fun!'

'How did you follow the instructions in French?' Andy asked.

'I just followed what everybody else was doing. They didn't know that I was English they just thought I was French. How's your romance, Andy?'

'We're planning the wedding. There seems to be so much to organise for one day, but we're getting there.'

'Wouldn't you just like to go off and get married in a registry office?' asked Angelina.

'Well, I would, but you know what relatives are like.'

'Hmmmm,' said Angelina.

'Did you have a white wedding, Ryta?'

'No, registry office.'

'Didn't you want a big do?'

'I feel the only people interested are those who are getting married; most of the relatives are often there just to make up the numbers.'

'Ryta, you're not being cynical, are you?' Roger asked.

'No, just realistic,' she answered promptly. 'Talking about cynical, what about the invitations now? Some state cash presents only. Here, read this invite I received today.'

We would like all the ladies to wear hats and for all the cars to sport wedding ribbons. We are not having a wedding list, but instead monetary contributions to our house-improvement fund would be greatly appreciated. Many, many thanks.

Parking for the services is behind the Parish Church in London Road; you will need a couple of pounds for the parking fee.

'This is the poem I have sent in return.'

Thank you for your invite to share your special day,
I wish you much happiness along your married way.
Thank you for specifying exactly what you need
In the way of presents, that's helpfulness indeed.
I know that tea and bath towels and all that other stuff
You've already bought and really have enough.
But it's not the small things that you want to receive now,
It's bathroom/kitchen suites or a holiday in Macau.
And as much as I would like to give these things to you
I'm saving very hard to replace my things too.
So sorry if my gift seems small, but it's all I've got,
But sell it on eBay and put the money in your pot!

After they'd all clapped, Andy said, 'Of course you are all invited. I have been very happy here.'

'The next time you call on a Sunday, come for dinner, and bring Cindy,' Ryta replied.

'Okay, I will!'

Back in the kitchen, the Colonel asked, 'Still writing, Ryta?'

'Yes, and I have been thinking back to what happened when I completed my first book.'

'What was that, dear?'

'I rang a medium friend who had regressed me twice, to ask him if everything that was needed had been put in the book. While we were on the phone, I was told clairvoyantly that when Mick, my ex-husband, and I were together in a previous lifetime, where he was a friar and I was a serf, Mick raped me. I asked Martin, the medium, why I should be given that information now, and he said, "Now is the right time for you to know. This time Mick has chosen to come back and be your husband, so it is payback time. It is the law of cause and effect, or what goes around comes around. After thirty years, you've said you don't want him any more and he now feels the rejection, hurt and humiliation that you felt when you were raped as a serf."'

Chapter 18
Andy

One wet afternoon, the doorbell rang, but before Ryta could answer it, the kitchen door opened.

Andy stood there looking pale and drawn, with red-rimmed eyes.

'Andy, are you ill?' Ryta asked as she stood to put the kettle on.

'No…' he said.

Then, in a low voice, as though the words were being pulled from deep inside him, he said, 'Cindy is dead.'

'Dead?' Ryta repeated. 'What happened?'

He sat down, his eyes devoid of emotion, and began the tale.

'When I got in from work last night, I found her collapsed on the floor. I tried to wake her but I couldn't; I dialled 999. The ambulance arrived ten minutes later and they took us to hospital, but she never regained consciousness. They said it was a brain tumour and there was nothing they could do.'

His lips trembled and his eyes filled with tears.

'Oh, Andy,' Ryta said, 'I'm so sorry.'

She put her arms around his shoulders as he began to sob.

'I've had to wait all this time to find someone I love and who really loves me, and now she's gone… I can't believe it.' He wept.

Ryta cried silently as she hugged him to her, feeling his anguish, anger and despair. Eventually, he stopped crying and placed his trembling hands round his mug of tea.

'How will I go on?' he asked.

'We all have lessons to learn, Andy. Lots of folk never experience a love like yours, so although you don't think so now, it is better to have loved and lost, than never to have loved at all. There must be a reason she was taken from you; she must have been a very special person and already learnt all her lessons.'

They both began to cry again.

'Just cry, Andy, let it all out; the tears will stop eventually.'

Chapter 19
A Positive Ending

There are lots of negative opinions about Facebook, of folk posting unimportant comments such as what they had for breakfast, but recently Ryta was told how it was extremely helpful to a lady in distress.

She had arrived at a festival to sell her crafts, as she made her own jewellery. She parked the car and then later found that it would not start. Her husband, who was a car mechanic, tried to fix it, but without success. They phoned a friend, but he too was unable to help.

Facebook came to the rescue. She posted the problem on her page and a kind lady follower posted in return that her husband was in the area, and if she sent her their postcode and car registration, he would be over as soon as possible.

The husband arrived, found the problem and fixed it! She now believes in the old adage: All the strangers in the world are merely friends we do not know.

The End.